CHOSEN BY GRACE

USA TODAY BESTSELLING AUTHOR
ALICIA RADES

Copyright © 2018 Alicia Rades

All rights reserved. No part of this book may be used or reproduced in any matter whatsoever without written permission from the author except in brief quotations used in articles and reviews.

This is a work of fiction. Names, characters, places, and incidents are either the product of the author's imagination or are used fictitiously, and any resemblance to actual persons, living or dead, business establishments, events or locales is entirely coincidental.

Published by Crystallite Publishing.
Produced in the United States of America.
Edited by Megan Linski.
Proofread by Emerald Barnes.
Cover design by Rebecca Frank.

To Megan. This series would be nothing without you.

Considering I'd been seeing demons my whole life, I should've expected one of those sons of bitches to attack someday. And maybe I would've—if I'd known they were real. I'd become so accustomed to assuming the cloaked figures were figments of my imagination that I eventually stopped noticing them. The problem with closing your eyes? Sooner or later, you have to open them again.

I squinted across the lawn toward the old white farmhouse. Music pumped from somewhere inside and reached us where we were parked near the road. Silhouettes of dancing teens passed the front window. A short distance from the house, a large group stood around a fire pit and threw their heads back in laughter. My eyes landed on a hooded figure immersed in the crowd.

My fingers froze against my dangly earring I'd been fidgeting with.

Usually, I didn't notice the figures, but this was the first one I'd seen since moving to Eagle Valley. I thought I was starting to get over the nightmares of my childhood.

"Is something wrong?" Allie pulled her gaze from the rearview mirror to look at me.

I continued to stare at the crowd, but the hooded man I'd seen had vanished.

Just my imagination, I told myself. That phrase had become my mantra since I was eight.

"Ryn?" Allie prodded.

I turned to her. "Everything's fine. I'm just waiting for you. You know, your reflection will be there when we get back."

Allie laughed and tucked her lipstick into her makeup bag. "I would hope so!"

She stole one last look in the mirror. Allie had a natural beauty that came with her tan skin and sleek black hair, thanks to her Asian heritage. She'd expertly outlined her striking brown eyes with black liquid liner, and she'd even added false eyelashes for the occasion.

My version of going all out was borrowing a flowy purple top from Allie and letting her curl my hair. I hadn't even bothered to swap out my tennis shoes for something fancy.

She finally abandoned her reflection. "Ready?"

I'd only been ready for the last two hours. "Yep."

We stepped out of the car into the chilly Minnesota night air. Allie tugged down on her skirt and started down the long gravel driveway like she was walking down a runway. I followed beside her, but my hips didn't sway in the same confident manner. It definitely had something to do with the four-inch heels she was wearing.

As we neared the fire pit, I noticed what looked like a freshman chugging a beer.

"Are you sure we won't get in trouble?" I asked.

Allie shook her head. "Mike's parents are away for the weekend, and we're far enough out of town that no one will call in a complaint."

The smell of pizza and alcohol hit my nose at the front door, and the music was so loud I could feel it vibrating through the walls. Allie took my hand so we wouldn't lose each other. My eyes landed on several people on our way to the kitchen. A nervous sensation hit my gut as we waded through the crowd.

"Hey, you made it!" A tall guy with dark hair and a slightly crooked nose held an arm out to Allie.

She leaned into him with a smile.

"This is Kyle!" she shouted above the music.

She'd mentioned him before, how they weren't officially dating but had a thing for each other. By the way she talked about him, you'd think he was a god. Even with his crooked nose, he was attractive enough to be mistaken for one, at least.

"How about a shot for my girls?" Kyle didn't wait for an answer. He placed two plastic shot glasses on the kitchen island and poured each one full of a green liquid.

I eyed it skeptically. "I'm okay, thanks."

"It's sour apple. You'll love it." Kyle pushed the drink toward me.

"No, really," I insisted. "My mom would *kill* me."

Allie bumped hips with me. "Your mom's not here, is she? Live a little!"

A smile crept across my face. Allie was right. Mom *wasn't* here to tell me what I could and couldn't do. I might as well take advantage of the freedom while I had the chance. I snatched up my glass and downed the shot in one gulp. It burned as it flowed down my throat. I gagged.

"That a girl!" Allie tipped the shot into her mouth and asked for another immediately.

Kyle poured her drink and then turned to the fridge and handed me a hard lemonade. "Maybe you'd prefer something a little tamer."

I brought the bottle to my lips and welcomed the sweet flavor.

"Hey," Allie called to a group of three across the kitchen. "Come meet Ryn. She's starting at Eagle Valley High this year."

"Hi." I waved to two girls and a guy nervously. I'd already forgotten their names by the time introductions were over.

Allie had dragged me to this party so I could get to know people before school. I'd be attending Eagle Valley High my senior year while Allie was enrolled in the private school in town, Galen High.

Mom and I never stayed in one place for more than a year, so I never let myself get too attached to anyone. The only reason I spent time with Allie was because I'd moved in next door last month and she insisted we hang out.

Allie took a beer from the fridge. Her eyes instantly lit

up when the song changed. "Oh my God. I love this song. We have to dance!"

She grabbed my wrist and dragged me toward the living room.

"Don't have too much fun," Kyle called after us.

"Don't worry," I laughed. "I'll bring her back in once piece."

Allie rolled her eyes.

"What?" I asked over the music.

She took a sip of beer. "Kyle. He's so protective."

"When are you going to make it official?" I swayed my body to the music.

Her brows shot up. "Ask *him*."

The room was so crowded that Allie and I nearly touched as we danced. Her eyes darted across the room.

She did a double take. "Creep alert, nine o'clock."

I glanced to my left. My eyes fell on a tall guy with ruffled brown hair standing alone in the corner. The music and chatter faded as our eyes connected. He had the strong jaw and perfectly symmetrical features of a movie star. Even from this distance, I could tell his electric blue eyes were worth getting lost in for hours.

Hot Stuff wore a leather jacket over his broad shoulders like he was some kind of badass biker dude. His lips curled into a slight smile the longer I held his gaze. He leaned against the wall as if amused and stuck a hand into the pocket of his tight jeans.

All I wanted him to do was turn around so I could see what those pants looked like from the back. He could get rid of the pants for all I cared.

My cheeks flamed at the thought. I turned back to Allie before I could completely undress him with my eyes.

"Cute guy? Leather jacket?" I asked.

"No, closer."

I checked my left again and found a muscular guy in a backwards baseball cap staring at us while he danced. As soon as he saw us look, he began making his way through the crowd.

"Do you know him?" I hissed in Allie's ear.

She shook her head. "I've seen him around. He goes to your school."

I quickly searched for an exit while Allie tried to work her way through the crowd casually, but we were squeezed too tight. The guy reached us far too soon.

"Hello, ladies." He dragged out the words and eyed us up and down.

"Um, hi," Allie said shyly.

Maybe I was too quick to judge, but based on what looked like a homemade tattoo on the guy's arm and the strong scent of alcohol on his breath, I could tell he wasn't the kind of guy either of us wanted to get involved with.

"Sorry, not interested," I said boldly.

Allie and I turned our attention back to each other and continued dancing like we never noticed his approach.

"Your friend here is *feisty*." He draped an arm around Allie's shoulder. The cup in his hand nearly spilled over the front of her blouse.

I cringed.

I grabbed Allie's arm and pulled her away from him,

though there wasn't really anywhere for us to go. "Sorry, but she's taken."

"I don't see anyone claiming her," the guy challenged with a laugh.

Allie shot me a pleading expression, begging me to save her from this guy. I did the only thing I thought would make him get lost. I wrapped an arm around her waist and pulled her into me. She continued dancing like the guy didn't bother her.

I gave him an extremely fake, exaggerated expression of apology. "Like I said, she's taken."

He glanced between us like he was trying to figure out if we were for real. "A two for one deal? That's hot."

I wanted nothing more than to slap the ugly smile right off his face. "That's not how this works."

"How can you not want a piece of this?" He gestured to his body, which wasn't very impressive.

My jaw tensed, but my serious expression never faltered. "I'm not interested in dicks."

I wasn't talking about anatomy, either.

Douchebag huffed and walked away like he'd never been turned down before.

As my eyes followed him, I noticed Hot Stuff had made his way halfway through the crowd. He stared straight at me like he'd planned on stepping in to teach Douchebag a lesson. I shot him a small smile to let him know we were okay and didn't need his help.

"Thank you." Allie breathed a sigh of relief. "That was brilliant."

I couldn't suppress my laugh. "Did you see the look on his face?"

She nodded. At the time, we both thought that was the end of it.

It wasn't until we were leaving that we spotted Douchebag again. Allie had so much to drink that I finally cut her off and told her we were going home. I'd have to figure out how to sneak her past her dad's room later.

I supported her weight on the way back to the car. A cool breeze sent my hair dancing in the wind.

"Hey," someone called when we passed the fire pit.

I didn't realize they were talking to us until they called again. We turned.

Douchebag stepped forward with a beer in his hand.

"Well, would you look who it is?" He covered his mouth with his fist, and the word *bitches* slipped out between coughs.

A few guys around him laughed.

"That's not very nice," Allie slurred.

"It's not nice to turn down a nice guy like me, either." He shifted his weight rather unevenly between his feet.

"You," Allie pointed, "are *not* a nice guy."

"Me?" he feigned. "You never gave me the chance. You don't know what you're missing."

Allie opened her mouth to say more, but I pulled her away.

"Come on," I whispered in her ear. "Let's get you home."

I thought ignoring him might be enough, but his footsteps followed. I slowed, not wanting to lead him to the car. My fists clenched at my sides.

"Come on, Tad," one of the other guys said.

"Where are you going?" Tad insisted. "Take me with you. We could throw a party for three."

Allie whirled around and stumbled over her own feet before I caught her. "*That's* how I know you're not a nice guy."

Tad stepped toward Allie and lowered his voice. "So maybe I *am* a bad guy. If you take me for a test drive, you might find out you like the flavor." He reached out and placed a hand on her exposed thigh.

My heart lurched in surprise. Before he could get his hand up her skirt, I slapped it away. Noises erupted from the guys around us. I couldn't tell if they were on my side or Tad's. I had the overwhelming urge to barf and punch the guy at the same time. I was *not* going to let him touch my friend like that.

The anger I'd been suppressing bubbled to the surface. My skin heated and sizzled with rage, and the air around us suddenly seemed charged with energy. I let Allie go and raised my arm, but before I could throw the first punch, everyone went silent.

Fear entered Tad's eyes. He backed away but tripped over his own feet and fell to the ground.

Everyone gaped at me. Even Allie, who had fallen to the earth without anyone to support her, stared at me wide-eyed.

"What?" I snapped.

Before anyone could answer, I glanced down at myself and noticed for the first time what they were all staring at.

A white glow danced across my fist and lit up my arm

like an electric charge. I opened my hand and tried to shake the substance off of it.

Bad idea.

A luminous white orb the size of a softball rose from my palm. My first thought was that I was hallucinating again, but I could tell by everyone's faces that I wasn't imagining it.

As soon as the shock overcame me, the orb disappeared, and my hand returned to normal. I scanned the crowd, hoping someone might be able to tell me what was going on. A dozen stunned faces stared back at me.

I noticed one guy in the back cloaked in a dark hood. A shiver ran down my spine, but I didn't have time to worry about whether I was imagining him or not. I had to get away from all those eyes and figure out what the hell was going on with my hand.

I turned to Allie and bent to help her up. Before I got her to her feet, a heavy weight crashed into me. The air left my chest, and I tumbled to the ground.

2

I rolled over to find Tad straddling me. Squeezing my eyes tightly shut, I expected the blow to come any second now.

Suddenly, his weight disappeared. My eyes opened, and I stared up at the dark, starless sky. The moon peeked out through the clouds.

I rose to a sitting position and immediately became alert when I saw two guys fighting in the grass to my left. The first thing I noticed about the second guy was his broad shoulders and leather jacket. My heart flipped in my chest.

Hot Stuff threw a punch. Before he could get in another one, Tad scrambled to his feet and ran off toward his friends.

My savior hurried over to where I sat and offered a hand to help me to my feet. In a silent mutual agreement, we both took one of Allie's arms and supported her weight as we distanced ourselves from the fire pit. Darkness enveloped us, leaving nothing but moonlight to guide us down the long driveway.

"Are you crazy?" he hissed. "In front of all those people? It's going to be fun explaining that one. You're lucky they're all drunk enough that we can convince them it was a trick of the light."

"What are you *talking* about?" I bit back through shallow breaths. "You think I did that on purpose?"

"You know you can't use essence to intimidate people. Have you not learned anything?"

I narrowed my eyes at him. "I don't know what you're talking about."

"*That.* Back there."

Oh, wow. That's helpful.

"I don't—ow! Allie, that was my foot," I complained.

She muttered an incomprehensible apology.

We reached the car, and I opened the back door. Allie climbed inside and melted into the seat.

I slammed the door and spun back toward him. "Who *are* you?"

"Who are *you?*" he demanded.

"I asked you first."

He hesitated. "James Marek. Most people call me Marek."

"Well, thanks for the help, but I think I can take it from here." All I wanted was to escape this place. Even the prospect of learning more about this guy couldn't make me stay.

I turned, but he caught me before I could get out of reach.

"Aren't you going to answer *my* question? I've never seen you around before," he said.

I jerked my arm away from him. "Of course not. I just moved here."

He stared at me like he expected me to say more. "What's your name?"

I wasn't sure I should answer, but I caved under the weight of his heavy stare. "I'm Ryn. And I'm leaving."

"Wait!"

The urgency in his tone made me stop.

"It's not like Davina drop out of the sky every day," he said. "I think I recognize essence when I see it."

I backed away from him. The cool metal of the car touched my skin.

"Are you insane?" My voice shook. *No, Ryn. You're the crazy one.*

"This is serious." Marek spoke through clenched teeth. "Do you know how much trouble you could get in for something like this?"

My pulse quickened, and my face grew hot. This had to be a dream or something. Maybe I drank more than I thought and had passed out.

"I think I can defend myself just fine," I said.

I started around the back of the vehicle toward the driver's side, but a second voice caught my attention.

"Maybe you should listen to your boyfriend."

I turned around, expecting Tad to be back. Instead, I found two cloaked figures approaching us. Their faces were hidden beneath the shadows of their hoods. My first instinct was to ignore them like I had my entire life. But when I glanced around and found no one else nearby, I realized the voice must've come from one of the dark figures.

That couldn't be right. They hadn't spoken to me in years.

Marek took a defensive stance.

"You can't see them, can you?" I asked him accusingly.

"Of course I can," he said, not taking his eyes off the men. Marek's tone shifted as he addressed them. "You don't want to try anything. Believe me."

The taller figure spoke first. "Little Angel looks fun to play with. How can we resist?"

The other man chuckled. "What do you think, Dorian? You take the guy, I'll take the girl?"

A muscle popped in Marek's jaw. "You shouldn't be here. You know you'll get yourself killed before you make it out of town."

"But it's so much fun when all you young angels gather together with no protection," the taller one said. "Your kind aren't the only ones who have fun killing. The fewer there are of you in the world, the better."

I inched away slowly, my hands shaking. Now would be a really good time to wake up.

"I wouldn't bet on that," Marek said.

Before I could process what was happening, a white light erupted from Marek's palm and hit the first man in the shoulder. He crumbled to the ground and lay on his back breathlessly.

"Oh my God! What did you do?" I tried to push past

Marek to check Dorian's pulse, but he grabbed my wrist and pulled me behind him.

The second man crossed in front of Dorian.

Marek faced him and spoke in a strong voice. "I wouldn't try anything if I were you, unless you want to end up like your friend."

A second ball of energy formed in Marek's palm. It glowed intensely like some sort of magical fireball.

"You think you're better than me?" the man challenged. He extended a hand out from underneath his cloak. A similar object appeared to grow from out of nowhere. His fireball had a dark black center outlined in a reddish white glow that contrasted against the darkness of the night. "What do you say we do this hand-to-hand? No essence."

"Only if you don't want to survive," Marek said confidently.

An icy laugh erupted from the man's chest. "Have it your way." He swung his hand around, sending the dark fireball flying in our direction.

I couldn't think fast enough to duck out of the way. Luckily, Marek spun around and tackled me to the ground. The black ball disappeared behind us.

Marek shuffled to his feet and lunged toward the figure. His fist connected with the guy's jaw. Before the second punch could reach him, the man caught Marek's fist and twisted his arm around. A loud thud came when he shoved Marek onto the hood of the car.

"Stop!" I cried, but my throat closed up around my words. My knees shook as I rose to my feet.

Marek gasped for breath. The man stood over him and squeezed his fingers around Marek's throat.

"Stop!" I pleaded again. "You're going to kill him." Fear stalled me from making a move.

The man only laughed.

Anger instantly replaced my fear. Blood rose to the surface of my skin, and a warm sensation spread to my fingertips. Another white fireball settled in my palm. My mind instantly flickered back to what Marek had done just moments ago when he threw something similar at the last guy. I drew my arm back and heaved the object at the man choking Marek.

The next few moments passed by in slow motion. The man glanced up at me. Surprised, he loosened his grip on Marek's throat and shifted to fight back.

Somewhere on its course to him, the white ball of energy transformed into a dark purple. He made a move to dodge the object, but before he could get out of the way, the purple ball of energy hit him in the chest. His cloak crumbled to the ground in a heap as his body vanished in a puff of black smoke.

This is not happening to me again.

I'd been so preoccupied with saving Marek that I hadn't realized Dorian had sat up. He glanced between where his friend had vanished and me.

Marek coughed and sucked in several breaths.

Another white fireball formed in my hand.

Dorian stood, and a black ball of energy rose from his own fingers. Marek placed his feet firmly between us.

Dorian hesitated for a moment and then closed his fist. The orb in his hand disappeared.

The light emanating from Marek's hand illuminated Dorian's face just enough that I could see his black irises. My gut twisted at the sight.

Dorian narrowed his inhuman eyes at me. "You shouldn't have done that, Little Angel. Now I know what you are, and—"

"You'll never get close to her," Marek said with conviction. "Not as long as I'm around."

Dorian scoffed. "You won't be around forever."

Marek's face twisted in anger. In one quick motion, he hurled his fireball at Dorian. Dorian spun out of the way, and the fireball exploded like a firecracker against the ground. Dorian snatched up his friend's cloak and rushed away from us, escaping into the darkness.

"Shit," Marek muttered under his breath. "He's going to be back. And it's going to be ugly."

3

*E*xhaustion sent me tumbling to my knees. Marek rushed to steady me and slowly lowered me to the ground. I closed my eyes and pressed my head against the cool metal of the car door.

I'm hallucinating again.

Why, then, did it feel so real?

I opened my eyes. Marek sat beside me with his elbows rested on his knees, breathing in deeply.

He must be part of the hallucination, I thought. It's not like sexy hunks showed up every day to rescue me from figments of my imagination.

"Are you okay?" Marek asked.

Physically? Yeah.

Mentally? Maybe it was time to check in with a therapist again.

I wasn't worried about myself, though. My main priority was getting Allie home safely.

"I'm fine, but I have to get my friend home." I rose to my feet. "I'll see you around."

"Wait."

I didn't. I slipped into the driver's seat and grabbed Allie's keys from the floor where she'd left them. My hand shook as I stuck the key in the ignition.

It felt strange being in the driver's seat again. Mom wouldn't let me drive after what happened the last time I got behind the wheel.

Marek grabbed my door before I could shut it. "You can't just *leave*."

"I can." I ripped the door from his grasp and narrowly missed squashing his fingers. Allie shifted slightly in the back seat at the sound of the slamming door.

"Seriously. This is a big deal." He knocked on the window.

I sighed and rolled it down. "Seriously, I have to get Allie home. Maybe we can talk about this later."

Marek gaped at me. "Let me come with you. You shouldn't be alone."

"I'm not. Allie's with me." Even if she wasn't exactly conscious.

"At least let me know how I can get in touch with you," he insisted.

I sighed. If I didn't give him something, he wasn't going to let me leave. I was too freaked out to stay.

"I'm staying at Allie's house."

"I can meet you there in the morning," he offered.

My brows shot up. "And you just happen to know where she lives?"

He nodded. "Yeah, we go to school together."

"Okay, I'll see you in the morning." I rolled up the window and shifted into drive. I had no intention of ever seeing Marek again.

I woke the following morning with a pounding headache and momentarily wondered where I was.

The first thing I noticed was the white vanity to my left, and then I spotted Allie's pink comforter hanging off the edge of her bed to my right. Allie's shoes were strewn at the floor near my feet. I'd taken them off for her last night and never bothered to put them away nicely. I still wore the same clothes I'd gone to the party in.

Allie stirred from the bed above me and cleared her throat. "How do you feel?"

"I'm fine," I lied. "You?"

"Like shit," she admitted. She attempted to sit up but immediately fell back onto her bed. "How'd we get home?"

"I drove you back and snuck you in."

"Thanks. I don't know what I would've done without you there. I'm so thirsty."

I climbed out of my sleeping bag and stood. "I'll get you some water."

"No," she insisted kindly. "I can do it."

"Relax," I told her. "You have a pretty bad hangover."

I walked out of the room before she could argue further. In the bathroom, I filled the glass next to the sink with water. My eyes landed on my hand as I twisted the faucet. I remembered the white orb forming in my palm so vividly. I'd never forget the deep purple it transformed into.

But things like this didn't happen in real life. There had to be another explanation. Had Kyle slipped something in my drink? It would explain my headache.

The cool water hit my skin as it spilled over the edges of the glass, pulling me from my thoughts. I immediately twisted the faucet off and returned to Allie's bedroom.

"Here you go." I handed her the glass.

She rolled over and thanked me.

"Hey, Allie. Kyle's cool, right?" I asked.

"What do you mean?" She sat up and sipped her water.

"I mean, he can be trusted, can't he? He wouldn't mess with someone's drink?"

"God, no. He'd never do that." Allie's eyes widened. "You think you were drugged? Because that douchebag—"

"No," I answered quickly.

Tad certainly seemed like a viable suspect, but he never got close enough to my drink to slip something in it.

"Do you know someone named Marek?" I asked.

She took another sip of water. "Yeah. We're in the same class at Galen. Why?"

"I met him last night."

Which meant everything had been real.

Holy shit. My knees shook so badly I had to sit in the chair next to her vanity to steady them. This changed everything I knew about my childhood.

"What'd you think of him?" Allie wiggled her eyebrows. "He's cute, right?"

"Huh?" My face flushed. "Yeah, he's cute. We didn't really talk much."

Allie wrinkled her nose. "Probably for the best."

I straightened. "What do you mean by that?"

Allie sighed and rested her drink in her lap. "He's just… a little too serious at times."

"Oh?"

"We're always in groups together in class," she explained. "I mean, we get along, but he can be kind of controlling. He thinks he's better than everyone else. Anyway, you don't want to get involved with anyone at Galen High. Dating someone from a different school is hard."

"I didn't say I wanted to date him!"

She giggled.

"I was just curious what his deal was and all."

Memories from last night flashed through my mind. Marek saw the cloaked figures. I wasn't alone.

Not to mention I can shoot freaking fireballs out of my hands.

I stood quickly. "I have to go."

"What? Why?" She asked in surprise.

I have to test out this fireball thing and confirm I'm not insane.

"I have chores." That wasn't exactly a lie.

"Okay." She relaxed. "See you later."

I grabbed my overnight bag from the floor. "Bye."

I left the house wondering how I was going to test what I'd experienced last night. Perhaps my anger at the time had something to do with it.

As soon as I stepped out of Allie's front door, my heart soared in my chest. At the end of her driveway stood the one thing that was sure to help me make sense of it all.

Marek leaned against a sleek black motorcycle looking even sexier than the first time I met him. He wore the same tight pants he had on last night, and his brown hair was tousled in the same manner. He'd draped his leather jacket over the handlebars of the motorcycle. Without it on, I had a great view of his thick biceps.

Heaven help me. I was undressing him with my eyes again.

Marek smiled at me, but it didn't quite reach his tired eyes. Had he slept at all? He stood there waiting for me like he'd camped out in Allie's yard last night.

"We need to talk," I stated as soon as I reached him.

He straightened. "Agreed."

"What the hell happened last night?" I demanded.

Marek gazed at me from under long lashes. "You really don't know?"

My brows shot up. "I really don't know. I mean… was it… real?"

A shocked expression crossed his face. "Of course it was real. What, you don't fight demons on a daily basis?"

My eyes widened. "You do that *all* the time?"

Marek chuckled. "No. We get idiots like that coming into town every now and then trying to show how tough they are."

"So, they're like… actually demons? From Hell?"

"No, that's just what we call them. Maybe we should go somewhere private to talk about it."

I glanced down the quiet residential street. It was completely deserted.

"It's private enough here. So, you can see them, too? I'm not the only one?"

He eyed me curiously for at least five seconds.

Say something already, dammit!

"You really have no idea?" he asked.

My mouth hung open, but nothing came out. *Uh, duh!*

Marek took my silence as an answer. "You're lucky I was there. I almost didn't come, but Kyle made me." He paused and pressed his lips together in thought. "I think I should introduce you to Fletcher."

My eyebrows pressed together. "Who's Fletcher?"

"He's the guy who can answer your questions. Should we get going?" Marek grabbed the helmet off his seat and shoved it into my hands.

"On *that* thing?" I squeaked.

"Why not?" he asked. "There's enough room for two."

"But there's only one helmet." I held it up to prove my point.

He slipped on his jacket and swung a leg over the bike. "That's why I gave it to you. Put it on."

I bit my lip nervously. I'd never ridden on a motorcycle before.

"Well?" Marek prodded. "Do you want answers or not?"

Mom didn't expect me home for hours, and I'd only ditched Allie so I could figure this all out. The answer was obvious.

But how did I know I could trust him?

Because he saved my life.

And there was nothing I wanted more than answers right now.

I shoved the helmet back into his hands. "Give me a second."

I hurried up my porch steps and dropped my overnight bag inside the front door. When I returned to the bike, Marek had his phone up to his ear.

"Okay," he said into it. "We'll see you soon."

He hung up and slid the phone into his back pocket.

"Here," he said, handing me the helmet.

"I don't need it." I pushed it back toward him.

"Yes, you do. I'd rather you wear it than me."

I was about to protest again, but then he reached for my hand. His touch was warm and electric.

Marek placed the helmet in my palm. "Put it on, Ryn."

If I knew hearing him say my name would melt my insides the way it did, I would've asked him to say it sooner.

I put the helmet on and swung my leg over the bike behind him. Not quite sure where to place my hands, I settled them on his shoulders. They shook in laughter.

"What?" I asked sharply. "Let's go."

"You've never ridden a bike before, have you?"

"No shit, Sherlock."

"Usually your arms go around my waist." He took my hands and pulled them around him.

My breath caught in my throat, and my entire body tensed. Shouldn't we at least go on a date before we got this close? I wouldn't know.

I could feel Marek's strong muscles under his shirt. My

heart hammered so hard I was sure he could feel it against his back.

Lovely. I was going to die of a heart attack.

The engine roared to life, and before I knew it, we were speeding down the street.

There was no telling what kind of trouble I was getting myself into.

4

*I*t took a moment for reality to sink in. I'd just hopped on the back of a stranger's motorcycle so he could take me God knows where. *What was I thinking?*

Marek drove so fast through the streets of Eagle Valley that a scream erupted from my lungs. I squeezed my eyes shut and wrapped my arms around him so tightly I thought I might crush his ribs. Instead of slowing like I wanted him to, he took it as an invitation to increase his speed.

Relief flooded through me when I felt him apply the brakes. I finally opened my eyes. We were in front of Galen High.

Three stories of red brick complete with white stone accents towered above us. The third floor was mostly slanted roof, but three peaks with small balconies housed extra windows for the top story. The Jacobean-style building featured five chimneys and a beautiful ornate window above the front doors. The only thing standing between us and the brick beauty was a vast manicured lawn bordered by a deciduous forest.

This place looked more like Galen Mansion than Galen High School.

I steadied myself against the bike when I dismounted it.

"Are you okay?" Marek asked. He reached out toward me, but at the last second, he pulled away.

"I'm fine." I slipped off the helmet and shook my hair out like that proved something.

I followed Marek up the sidewalk to the front entrance. Each step closer to the school had me questioning my sanity. I tried to reassure myself I was safe. Aside from a middle-aged woman jogging across the road with earbuds in, the street was quiet. I had to remind myself I was doing this for answers.

Marek sat on the top step. "We'll have to wait for Fletcher to unlock the door."

I took a seat beside him. Just when I opened my mouth to ask more about this Fletcher person, Marek spoke again.

"So, tell me about yourself."

I felt a blush rise to my cheeks and tucked a strand of brown hair behind my ear. He couldn't actually be interested in getting to know me.

"What do you want to know?" I asked.

He shrugged. "How have you grown up your whole life not knowing what you are?"

Good question. "You mean, not knowing I could shoot fireballs out of my hands?"

"They're not fireballs," he said with a laugh, "but yeah. Are you adopted or something?"

The question caught me off guard. "No. Why would you say that?"

"I'm sorry. I just figured your parents would tell you—"

"Well, they didn't," I bit harshly. I took a deep breath to steady my tone. "My mom definitely doesn't know about any of this." If she did, she wouldn't have taken me to three different therapists by the time I was eight. "I guess it's possible my father knew..."

"But?" Marek prodded curiously.

I wasn't sure why I opened up to him. Part of me said it was because I wanted answers and figured the more I shared, the more he'd share. Another part of me suspected it was his inviting smile. Something about him held an air of trustworthiness.

"My dad has never been around," I told him vaguely. "He left before I was born."

"Oh," Marek said simply, dropping his gaze to his feet. I could tell he regretted asking the question. "So, what brought you to Eagle Valley?"

Silence settled once again as I considered the question. I remained quiet for so long that I was sure Marek was wondering if I'd actually answer.

"I did," I finally said.

He tilted his head in question.

"My mom and I move a lot," I explained. "She's always on the search for a new adventure. She can't stay in one place for too long. It's like no place is ever good enough for her."

I didn't mention why I thought that was. Mom would never admit it, but I suspected deep down, she hoped to someday run into my father again.

"Mom usually chooses where we'll go next," I said. "This time, she let me choose."

"Why Eagle Valley, though?" Marek asked.

"Fate, I guess." It was the only thing that made sense. Coincidence didn't just land you in the lap of a dreamy guy with all the answers, did it? "When Mom said I could choose, I knew I wanted to move to the Midwest. I've always loved it here. It's so green in the summer, and I love the snow in the winter. But I didn't really care what part of the Midwest we moved to, so I tacked a map to the wall and threw a dart at it. It landed on top of Eagle Valley."

Marek pressed his lips together and nodded, considering the information.

"Aren't I the one who's supposed to be asking the questions?" I teased.

He shot me a smile.

Dayum. He could smile at me any time he wanted.

"What do you want to know?" he asked.

"If those things were demons, what are we?"

Before he could reply, the sound of an approaching vehicle stole both of our attention. The gray crossover pulled into the school parking lot across the street and parked in the closest space.

Marek stood. "That's Fletcher. He'll be able to answer your questions."

A thin man with gray hair stepped out of the vehicle. He wore tan slacks and a blue button-down shirt. A messenger bag bounced against his hip as he rushed up the walkway. He stuck his hand out in my direction when he reached us. I shook it.

"Samuel Fletcher," he introduced himself. He sounded slightly winded like he was in a hurry. "Most students simply call me Fletcher. You must be Ryn. James told me about what happened last night."

I was about to ask who James was before remembering it was Marek's first name.

Fletcher stepped past us and stuck a key in the front door. He held the door open for us while he spoke. "He says it gave you quite a shock."

An uncontrollable laugh bubbled up from my chest. "You could say that."

I fell silent the moment I stepped through the doors. The architecture inside was even more spectacular than the exterior.

A large foyer opened to the second level, where a balcony overlooked the commons area. Plush sofas and chairs surrounded a massive antique fireplace to our right. To our left sat a large staircase with a dark walnut banister. The same wooden texture covered the floors and bordered the doorways. Even the white walls and ceiling featured carved wooden accents.

Hints of a lemon-scented cleaner filled the air, but it couldn't completely cover the smell that reminded me of an old museum. There was nothing modern about this building, but it contained a unique charm that made me feel at home.

"You're kidding me," I blurted as I took in the scene.

"This place is a school?"

"It is now. It used to be a mansion," Fletcher explained. "It belonged to the brothers who founded Eagle Valley. My room is this way."

I followed behind him, but my attention remained on the architecture. Fletcher led us under the balcony and to a hall behind the grand staircase. I stole a glance inside a pair of open doors directly across from the front entrance. It was a small cafeteria dotted with dark wooden tables that matched the rest of the antique décor.

We entered a wide hallway and took the second door on the right. Three short rows of student desks faced a large desk at the front of the room. A modern whiteboard hung on the wall behind it.

"It's unfortunate you had to find out this way, but I'll explain the best I can." Fletcher dropped his bag on his desk and fell into the chair behind it so hard that it rolled across the floor a few inches. "Please, have a seat."

I followed Marek's lead and sat in one of the desks in the front row. My heart hammered quicker than I would have thought possible as I anxiously awaited answers.

"So… um…" I couldn't get the words out. Where did I even start? "Any idea what's happening to me?"

Fletcher straightened in his chair. "Well, it appears you're a Davina."

"What—what does that mean?" I tried to keep an open mind. "Am I, like, an alien?"

Both Marek and Fletcher laughed.

"Of course not," Fletcher said.

"So, what's a Davina?" If possible, my pulse grew even

louder in my ears. "All I heard last night was something about angels and demons. I figured I was insane. But if Marek saw it all too…"

"We're not angels or demons," Fletcher said like he wasn't pleased with the terms. "We're similar, but the stories have it all wrong."

"So, you're not aliens or angels. Mutants?" This whole place definitely gave off an Xavier Institute vibe.

Fletcher smiled in amusement. "No, Ryn. We're where the stories of angels and demons came from, but we prefer not to use the terms as we have no religious affiliations. Not with any modern religion, anyway."

I glanced between the two of them. They stared back as if expecting me to take their word for it.

"Davina have been around much longer than humans have," Marek explained. "Unfortunately, so have the demons." He said the word *demons* with an air of disgust.

"I thought you said this wasn't an angels and demons sort of thing," I pointed out.

"Not like you're used to," Marek said.

"It's an insult," Fletcher clarified. "They're really called Aedes."

Uncertainty crossed my face. These guys must've been as crazy as I was.

"Who all knows about this?" I asked. "Everyone in Eagle Valley?"

"Oh, no," Fletcher said seriously. "We'd never reveal our secret. It's our duty as Davina to protect humans from the Aedes. We'd much rather they live in peace not knowing what was out there. We'd prefer not to cause a panic, and frankly, most of us aren't keen on the idea of becoming lab rats. Our secrets are kept within the walls of Galen High."

"Everyone at Galen knows?" I asked in shock.

"It's a Davina-only high school," Marek confirmed.

Holy shit. Allie went to Galen High. My best friend was an angel.

And here I thought I'd made normal friends this time.

"Here, and at other schools like ours, our students learn how to use their Davina skills," Fletcher explained. "Many of them go on to become Protectors and leave Eagle Valley to fight the Aedes. Eventually, most return to raise families, and we move on to training the next generation."

I remained quiet as I let the information sink in. How could *I* be a Davina? How could anything they were saying be true?

It can't be, I thought to myself. *It's all one big prank to psych out the new girl.*

"Show me that thing again," I demanded. I stuck my palm up in Marek's direction and wiggled my fingers.

He eyed me like he didn't know what I was talking about.

"The fireball thing," I said.

"I told you; they're not fireballs." Marek stretched out his palm, and a glowing white orb appeared.

I couldn't take my eyes off it. The longer I stared, the more I realized other colors swirled inside it. Though they were subtle, it was mesmerizing.

Fletcher stood and popped the cap off a marker. He began to write on the whiteboard like he was teaching a high school history lesson. "It's called essence. The Davina believe there are four energies that make up a person: their body, their life force, their consciousness, and their essence. The four are all interconnected and work together to create balance."

He drew lines on the board connecting each of the words. "The body is obvious. Life force is most closely tied to the body. It's the energy that keeps the body living. Consciousness refers to a person's thoughts. So, what's left?"

It took me a moment to realize he wanted me to answer. I stared up at the four words he'd written.

"Essence," I answered. *Whatever that means.*

"Right," Fletcher said. "But what *is* essence?"

How am I supposed to know?

I stared at him blankly.

"It's your *soul*," Fletcher said passionately. "It's your character, who you are as a person."

My eyes widened, and my words came out in a rush. "The fireballs are part of your *soul*? What happens when you throw one at someone? Are you throwing away part of your soul?"

What had I gotten myself into?

"No, no," Fletcher said quickly. "They're only a physical manifestation of your essence energy. It can be recharged."

Good to know.

"If a person's body is damaged and their life force severed, their essence returns to the earth to be used by later generations," Fletcher continued. "Essence is the only thing that survives after death."

I paused for a moment to think about it. "So, it's like reincarnation?"

Fletcher pressed his lips together in thought. "In a sense. Your energy gets recycled."

I took a moment to let this sink in. "Where do the demons fit in to this?"

"Good question." Fletcher returned to his chair.

I knotted my hands in my lap. How could this really be happening to me?

Fletcher began to recite the story like he'd told it a hundred times. "In the beginning, there were gods with unimaginable power. The gods yearned for children, but only the highest gods, called Divinities, were afforded the privilege. Their children didn't inherit all of their powers to begin with, and they didn't want the lesser gods diluting that power. Wanting the best for their children, the higher gods created a paradise they called Vehena. They gifted this realm to their children, the Davina.

"The lesser gods, known as Sanctities, saw what the Divinities had and began having their own children in secret. Their children were called the Aedes. When the secret got out, the Divinities called for the Aedes' execution. They believed their lack of power was an abomination, and they were furious that the Sanctities had broken the laws of their realm.

"The Sanctities begged for mercy and to spare the lives of their children. The Divinities agreed, but the arrangement didn't work out like the Sanctities hoped. Instead of sharing the god's realm or allowing the Aedes into Vehena, the Divinities stripped the Aedes of their immortality and marked them with darkness so they would never forget the sins of their fathers."

I glanced to Marek to see if he was buying all this. He stared up at Fletcher with a look in his eyes that told me he believed every word of it.

Fletcher continued. "The Divinities banished the Aedes to a dark, desolate realm called Malum. But even the gods couldn't stabilize the gateways between realms, and the Aedes returned.

"To remind everyone how powerful they were, the Divinities laid upon the Aedes a second curse. They could return to the god's realm, but they could do nothing but walk the realm and observe. Aside from the ground at their feet—and, of course, the Divinities and Davina—they could only interact with objects that originated outside the realm. Anything they brought from their realm wouldn't truly exist here. Their curse served as a constant reminder that this realm was not their home."

Fletcher took a breath. "The Sanctities were also cursed. They couldn't see, hear, or interact with their children or anything from their realm. This was to prevent alliances and keep the Sanctities from having more children. It was another way for the Divinities to exercise their power."

The Divinities sounded like a bunch of jackholes.

"This was the worst curse of all," Fletcher said. "It sparked a war, and the gods destroyed each other. The earth was what was left from the ashes of their realm."

"Shut up." I couldn't help it when the words flew from my mouth. "You're saying *gods* used to live on the earth?"

Fletcher nodded. "It was their realm before it was ours. After the dust settled, the earth acted as a bridge between Vehena and Malum."

And I was just supposed to believe in this religious nonsense?

Marek must've noticed the disbelief written on my face. "Let him finish the story," he whispered.

Fletcher cleared his throat. "The Davina had nothing to do with the Great War, and so they sought to form an alliance with the Aedes. The Davina didn't agree with the actions of their parents. They wanted to set things right again. To solidify their alliance, the Davina tried to bring back the Sanctities and reunite them with their children. They called upon the power in the sands of the earth, but instead of bringing the Sanctities back, a new race—the humans—were formed. The curse of the Sanctities remained."

"That's why humans can't see demons or their cloaks?" I interrupted. "Because of that curse?"

Fletcher nodded. "Precisely. In a sense, humans were created from what remained of the Sanctities, but they didn't possess any of their divine powers."

Goodbye, science.

"The Davina grew to love the humans," Fletcher said. "Several mated to create human-Davina hybrids that possessed the power of the Davina. That's where *we* come from."

"Except we're not as powerful as the original Davina," Marek clarified.

"Correct," Fletcher agreed. "Much of our Davina power

has been bred out throughout the generations. We're a closer match for the Aedes now. They're getting tougher to defeat."

"You're at war?" I asked.

Fletcher nodded. "Since the dawn of civilization."

Seriously, what the heck was going on? I was being introduced to a whole new religion here. What if I didn't want to be a part of this?

I shot up out of the desk. "I—I'm sorry."

I took one look at Marek's shocked expression and knew I'd never find the words to explain myself. I did the only thing that made sense in that moment.

I bolted.

5

"Ryn, stop," Marek called down the hall.

My breath hitched as he caught my wrist and whirled me around to face him. I jerked my hand out of his grasp, but he only reached for me again.

"Stop it!" I struggled against him and accidentally elbowed him in the ribs. Hard.

I broke free and raced to the end of the hall and turned to the right. Before I could get my hand on the front door handle, Marek slipped in front of me and blocked my path. I ran straight into his chest and nearly tripped over his feet.

I stumbled back. "What's your problem? Are you planning to keep me prisoner here or something?"

His gaze dropped. "No, I just think you need to hear more before you run off. Believe me. I felt the same way when I first came here. There's so much more you need to know."

I crossed my arms and pursed my lips. "My whole

40

world is being turned upside down, Marek. Everything I thought I knew… I just want the demons to go away."

He spoke softly. "I know. I can't make them go away, but I can promise you one thing."

I dropped my arms to my side. "What's that?"

"You'll never have to be alone in this again."

I didn't know how long we stood there staring at each other. It could've been just moments or half an hour. The look in Marek's eyes begged me to accept my new reality. And I knew I would, because he'd been right. I wasn't alone anymore.

"Should we sit down?" Marek offered, gesturing to the plush chairs by the fireplace.

Before I could agree, Fletcher's voice came from behind me. "Maybe we should give her some time to think about things."

I turned to look at him. He stood next to the banister with his hands crossed in front of him.

He stepped forward with a sympathetic expression on his face. "It's a lot to take in. Perhaps you should take the day to come up with a list of questions. Maybe later next week we can go over some of the basics, get you introduced to things a little before school starts."

It took me a long moment to process the implication of his words. "You mean, you want me to attend Galen High?"

A smile twitched at Fletcher's lips. "How else do you expect to learn how to use your skills?"

"I—I…" I didn't know what to say.

"Perhaps it's best if someone escorts you home," Fletcher suggested.

"Shouldn't we tell her about—?" Marek started to say, but Fletcher cut him off.

"I think we should take this slowly. You know what can happen if we spring too much information on a person too fast." Fletcher turned his attention to me. "Are you going to be okay?"

I thought about it for a second and shrugged. "I don't know."

"I'll come by on Monday to see how you're doing," Fletcher offered. "We can discuss your enrollment then."

"Okay, thanks."

When no one said anything else, I turned to the doors beside me and slipped out into fresh air. It had become warmer in the short time I'd been inside, and the air was dense with humidity, causing my shirt to cling to my skin. Though it was muggy and unpleasant, my head began to clear once I stepped outside. I was already to the end of the walkway when I heard Marek calling my name.

"Wait up, Ryn."

I stopped and turned to him. My hair danced in the light breeze.

"Do you want a ride home?" he asked.

"Oh, I—um..." I glanced to his bike. "No, it's okay. I'll walk."

Marek's brows shot up. "You sure you can find your way back?"

"Yes," I lied.

It was only when he pointed it out that I realized I wasn't sure how to get home. When Allie had shown me around town, we spent the whole day walking. All the landmarks blended in my mind. Plus, I hadn't been watching this morning when Marek drove me here.

I could tell by the smirk on Marek's face that he knew I wasn't telling the truth.

"Well, maybe not exactly," I admitted, "but I know the general direction, and Eagle Valley isn't very big. I can't exactly get lost."

"Get on the bike. I'll drive you home."

The tone in his voice told me I didn't have a choice. At least he'd save me time wandering around aimlessly.

"Yeah, okay," I caved.

He drove slower this time but still made me wear the helmet. Relief washed over me as soon as we made it to my street.

Marek didn't part with me at the curb like I thought he would. Instead, he followed me up the creaky wooden steps to the front door. He stared down at me with a hint of a smile. His eyes danced around my face like he expected an invitation inside.

My cheeks heated under his gaze. "What?"

"I just want to make sure you're all right."

My heart fluttered. It was nice for someone to actually care.

"It's all so scary, Marek," I admitted.

"I know." He truly sounded like he meant it. "I can help you if you let me. Let me give you my number. Then you can call me when you're ready."

I pulled my phone from my back pocket and handed it to him. He programmed his number in and gave it back.

"Do you have more questions?" he asked.

"I do." The problem was there were questions I was afraid to ask. "Later, though."

I pushed past him and into the house.

In the following silence, I glanced around the house, letting the light filtering in through the stained-glass window by the stairs distract me. That was one thing I liked about this house. It had character, from the big brass door handles to the ancient hardwood flooring. I was always finding something new in this house that gave it a bit of character.

After a deep breath, I dragged myself into the living room and fell onto the couch. I closed my eyes. If I could just fall asleep, maybe this would all be over.

This is really happening. It will never be over.

Several minutes later, a knock sounded at the front door. I sighed heavily and rose, wondering what Marek could possibly want from me.

But it wasn't Marek. It was Allie.

6

"Hey," Allie said softly. "How are you doing?"

I caught a glimpse of Marek retreating down the street on his bike. "He told you?"

Her face fell. "Yeah. You don't mind if I come in, do you?"

"No." I opened the door wider. "Are you feeling any better?"

"A little," she told me. Even with a hangover, she'd found enough energy to flawlessly reapply her makeup.

I led Allie up the stairs to my room. I knew she'd want to talk about what happened, but I didn't know how to approach the topic.

Allie entered the room behind me and glanced around. "You haven't finished unpacking yet?"

I followed her eyes. The white walls were bare, but I hadn't left any packing boxes lying out. "I did finish unpacking."

"Oh," she said. "I don't see any pictures or anything."

"I have pictures!" I defended. I sat on the bed and pointed to the framed photo on my dresser.

Allie walked over to it to get a better look.

"It's from when I was in seventh grade," I told her. "Just after Mom and I ran our first half marathon. That was when she was going through her fitness phase. It was right before her photography phase. Here, I'll show you."

I hopped up from the bed and crossed over to my closet. I pulled a thick scrapbook from the top shelf and handed it to Allie. She gazed down at it curiously and sat on my bed to flip through it.

"Oh, wow," she said in amazement. "These pictures are really nice."

"Yeah, but they're all from junior high. Like I said, my mom was going through her photography stage and photographed *everything*. And that led right into her scrapbooking phase."

Allie never took her eyes off the book. "Your mom's a really interesting person. She's talented at a lot of stuff."

I wouldn't exactly say *talented*.

I took a seat beside Allie. "She never sticks with one thing."

"What other kinds of things has she done?" she asked as she flipped through the pages.

"Mm…" I thought. "We had a martial arts phase and a cooking phase. Then obviously we had the running one and the photography and scrapbooking. She tried sewing once, but that didn't last long. For a year, all she did was read books. She read something like three hundred books that year."

Allie's eyebrows shot up. "Wow."

I'd never been impressed. It was like nothing could ever please my mom.

"What about you?" Allie asked.

"What do you mean?"

"What are you into? Are you like your mom, always changing your hobbies?"

I sighed heavily. "You know we move around a lot. I never get to be a part of anything for long. I was in martial arts classes for a few years in elementary school, and I played softball in junior high."

I shrugged. The truth was, Mom changed hobbies so often that I never had much of a chance to pursue my own interests. We didn't have the money for it. Her job as a virtual assistant didn't exactly pay a whole lot.

"I like cooking," I said. "That was my favorite phase she went through. Oh, and earrings! I *love* earrings."

I jumped up from the bed and pulled open the drawer at my desk. Allie closed the scrapbook and stood. When she saw my collection, she drew in an audible breath.

"I noticed you wore different earrings almost every day," she said, "but I never thought you'd have *this* many."

I smiled and opened the next two drawers, each displaying another set of my collection. Allie's eyes grew even wider.

"It looks like a lot because I keep the packaging for all of them so they don't get mixed up," I told her.

"It's still pretty cool," she said. "Have you checked out Celeste's yet?"

I shook my head. "What's that?"

"It's a jewelry store in town. I think you'd like it. It's on Main Street right next to Angela's Café. We should go sometime."

"Sounds like fun," I agreed.

I noticed I was still wearing the same dangly cubic zirconia earrings from the night before. I slipped them off and stuck them back where they belonged. I swapped them out for a pair of dark purple studs.

Allie sat on my bed. "Ryn, we need to talk. Marek told me about what happened last night. I wish I could've seen it."

I turned to her from where I sat in front of my mirror. "You saw part of it."

Allie sheepishly dropped her gaze. "I don't remember much of last night. I am *so* sorry I wasn't there for you. I didn't know about you. I never thought you'd be in danger. I never thought *any* of us would be in danger, not here."

"So I guess it's true, then. You're a Davina?" The word felt strange on my tongue.

Allie nodded. "Yeah. I can't believe you're one, too. Marek said you never knew."

"It's… definitely a surprise. I'm still trying to process it all."

Allie looked at me with a sympathetic expression. "I can't imagine not knowing."

I thought back to my childhood, wondering how things would be different if I knew. Would I have faced the demons sooner? What if I hadn't grown up thinking I was crazy?

"What was it like for you, growing up?" I asked curiously.

Allie twisted her lips in thought. "I don't know. It's always been normal for me."

"Could you always do that fireball thing?"

"You mean, conjure essence?" Allie stuck out her palm. A white fireball formed in it and floated just millimeters from her palm.

I stared at it, mesmerized.

She closed her hand into a fist, and the ball of energy disappeared inside it. "No, not always."

"How'd you learn how to do it?" I held out my hand and concentrated, but it remained empty. "You make it look so easy."

Allie shrugged. "I don't know. You just… do it."

"Is that how you learned? You just… did it?"

"Kind of," she admitted. "It should come naturally by now. The ability to manipulate essence comes later in our teens, after puberty. That's why we don't start our training until high school. Your essence is always there; you just can't access it until later."

"But if you don't develop your powers until your teens, how come…" My voice trailed off. I'd conjured essence once before when I was little, although I didn't know what had happened at the time. I wasn't sure if I should tell Allie about it.

"What is it?" Allie prodded. "It's okay, Ryn. I'll answer any questions you have. That's what friends are for." She gave an encouraging smile.

"If you don't develop your powers until later, how have I been able to see the demons my whole life?"

Allie suppressed a giggle. "All Davina can see demons. They probably left you alone until now because they never knew you were a Davina. They can't tell the difference between us and humans. Unless you show your essence or make eye contact, they wouldn't know."

I pressed my lips together. I didn't dare mention to her that they hadn't *always* left me alone.

"What?" Allie asked, sensing I had more to say.

I paused for a beat. "There don't seem to be many demons here in Eagle Valley."

It was one of the first things I noticed when we came here. I thought it meant I was finally growing out of my insanity.

"Of course not. There are far too many Davina here. They'd get themselves killed."

"Then what about the two last night?"

Allie dropped her head. "They were idiots. Sometimes the brave ones will stumble into town for fun. They don't usually make it very far."

I nodded. "Marek mentioned that."

"You're lucky he was there," she said seriously. "I wouldn't want to face a demon on my own."

I opened my mouth to ask more questions, but I cut off when my door opened.

"Kathryn, I'm headed to the store—" Mom stopped as soon as she saw Allie. "Oh. I saw your bag downstairs. I knew you were home, but I didn't realize... Are you coming to the store with me? I want to find some more yarn for that afghan I'm making."

Mom's latest thing was crocheting. If you asked me, it was a waste of time and money. She'd never stick with it.

"No, that's okay," I said.

"Why not? I thought you had fun the last time we went."

Where'd she get that idea? I hated yarn shopping. It was so dull, and the craft stores were always filled with that sickening scent like someone had lit too many candles.

"Mom," I complained. "I have a friend over."

She huffed like she couldn't believe I'd rather spend time with Allie than with her. "If you're going to stay home, I expect your chores to be done by the time I get back."

"Fine," I reluctantly agreed.

"Bye, Mrs. Tyler!" Allie called after my mom.

"Ugh. Don't call her that. It sounds weird."

"Sorry. Should I just call her Gloria?"

"Yeah, I guess that works." I stood from the bed. "I'm sorry, but I have a ton of cleaning to do before my mom gets home."

"I'll help you," she offered.

"You really don't have to do that." I didn't want to take advantage of her.

"Yes, I do," she insisted. "The sooner you get your chores done, the sooner I can teach you to manipulate your essence. You'll need to learn how to defend yourself. Should we get started?"

7

$\mathcal{A}$llie thought it best if we practiced somewhere with more space than my bedroom. After we finished cleaning, I took a shower and grabbed some lunch. I sent Mom a text letting her know I was hanging out with Allie the rest of the day.

I stared out the passenger side window of Allie's car. The bright sun from earlier had disappeared behind a layer of clouds. I wasn't sure where we were going until I noticed the red brick of Galen High at the end of the street.

"How are we going to get into the school?" I asked.

I wondered if maybe there was a back door that was easy to jimmy open with the right tool. That's how the seniors at my last school got in for their senior prank. They'd covered the entire gym floor in balloons.

"We're not going inside," Allie said simply.

"Where are we going, then?"

"It's behind the school."

52

I hesitated. "I don't think that's a good idea, Allie. I don't want anyone to see us."

"Don't worry. They won't," she said with a knowing smile.

Allie parked the car and led me around the side of the building into a forest of dense trees.

I followed behind her and kept my eyes on the dirt path. "Are you sure no one will see us?"

"Relax," she insisted. "This is at the edge of town, and the land belongs to the school. No one comes here who isn't supposed to. We use this place to train all the time."

"Fletcher said you train to become Protectors?"

"Yeah."

"What's a Protector, exactly?" I asked.

"They're like soldiers," she explained, "but Protectors usually work alone or in small groups so they don't draw attention. They kill demons."

"Kill them?" I asked warily.

Allie glanced back at me but didn't slow her pace. "Well, yeah. Demons feed off human essence. We protect them from that. Didn't Fletcher tell you?"

I stared down at my feet. "We didn't get that far. But it makes sense."

That didn't mean I wanted to have a hand in killing them, though.

"What if you don't want to become a Protector?" I asked.

"The Davina Council will assign you another job."

I relaxed slightly. "The Davina have their own government?"

"Mm-hmm."

"What kind of jobs do they assign?" I'd always thought it'd be cool to be a chef. I wondered if there were any options for that in the Davina world.

Allie shrugged. "Teaching, keeping track of records, protecting ancient Davina artifacts, things like that."

"And you?" I asked curiously. "You're planning to become a Protector?"

"Yeah," Allie said like it was obvious. "Most Davina start out as Protectors and then go on to teaching or whatever once they get older. It's kind of frowned upon to never become a Protector."

Lovely. I never thought I'd be able to list *soldier* on my résumé.

"Allie, are you sure this is the right way?" I complained.

The forest was so thick and dark that I was sure no one would see us out here. The only problem was there didn't seem to be any room off the path to practice much of anything except dodging overgrown roots.

"It's not much farther," she promised.

Just as she said it, I noticed a break in the trees ahead.

"Is that it?" I pointed.

She glanced back at me with a smile. "Yep. You're going to love it."

We stepped out of the trees and into the vast clearing. My eyes widened at what I saw.

We stood at the top of a large hill taller than any building in town. The base of the valley extended the length of several football fields, and the grass below us had been well manicured. The entire valley was surrounded by vibrant green trees at its highest points. It looked like something straight out of a Costa Rica travel magazine, only on a much smaller scale.

All it needed was a little log cabin at the base of the hill. Then, when I made my millions as a celebrity chef, I'd retire here.

My jaw dropped. "I can see why you train here."

"Right?" Allie agreed enthusiastically. "No one will ever see us."

To our right sat a stretch of wooden steps. I headed for the stairs, but Allie quickly stopped me.

"Don't be lame!" She lowered herself to the ground. Before I could ask her what she was doing, she began rolling down the hill on her side, tumbling over and over again.

"Allie!" I called.

Her laughter echoed throughout the valley.

"Be careful," I yelled.

Her voice rang back. "As… you… wish…"

I couldn't help but laugh at her *Princess Bride* reference. I took a deep breath and sat on the grass below me.

"Here goes nothing…"

I lay down on my side, spreading my arms above my head. Then I let my body tip until gravity took over and I could no longer control my momentum. Hysterical laughter erupted from my lungs as the world tumbled around me faster than I thought possible. My laughter turned into screams as my speed increased. What seemed like far too soon, I slowed and came to a halt at the base of the hill. My head spun as I pushed myself up.

"Crazy fun, right?" Allie asked from several yards away where she was still recovering.

A wide smile spread across my face. "So much fun. Can we do it again?"

And we did. We raced up the stairs. My legs burned, and my face flushed. Allie insisted we lie head-to-head and hold hands. We could've only been holding on for a few seconds before the momentum was too strong and our fingers slipped from each other's grips.

At the bottom of the hill, our laughter filled the valley. I stared up at the spinning sky, taking in the strange sensation. I felt unstable, almost like I was flying. I had this urge to do it again, only instead of rolling down the hill, I wanted to jump off it and spread my arms, hoping they would hold me up.

Obviously, that wasn't going to happen.

Allie hopped to her feet and ran her fingers through her hair. Bits of grass fell out of it and back to the earth. "You ready?"

I stood and dusted the dirt off my jeans. I couldn't help but feel slightly disappointed that she'd put a stop to our fun, but I needed to focus. If I could get the hang of this, maybe I could make sense of all the madness.

"How does this work?" I asked.

Allie extended her hand to demonstrate. "Think of it like flexing a muscle. It's something you just tell yourself to do, and you do it."

"Okay," I said.

This is never going to work.

I held out my arm, imagining the orb growing out of it

like Allie was doing. I flexed my fingers, working my muscles all the way up through my bicep and to my shoulder. My hand remained empty.

"It's okay. You've got this," Allie encouraged.

I narrowed my eyes as if my fingers might combust by sheer will. Eventually, I found myself tensing every muscle in my body. Not so much as a flicker entered my outstretched palm. A headache began to form.

"Relax," Allie instructed. "Don't think about it so hard."

I resisted the urge to roll my eyes and ask how I was supposed to do that. Instead, I gave in and released the tension in my muscles. Still, nothing happened.

I dropped my hand. "It's not working."

"I'm sorry. Maybe I'm just a bad teacher." Allie frowned.

My heart sank.

"No, it's not that," I assured her. "I'm probably a bad student."

Allie shot me a half-hearted smile. "I have an idea."

She held out her hand, and a white fireball formed in it without a single sign of struggle.

"Hold out your hand," she instructed.

I did, but I immediately recoiled when she reached out toward me.

"Don't worry," she said. "It's not going to hurt. I promise."

Warily, I let her take my hand. I *did* trust her, but that didn't keep my arm from shaking. Slowly, Allie raised her right hand above mine and tipped it until the fireball inside fell into my outstretched palm.

My fingers warmed for a mere second, and hope surged

throughout my chest, but the sensation immediately dissipated. The orb vanished as if it was made of mist.

"Dang it," Allie said. "I thought that might give you an idea of what it feels like. I thought it'd be easier to sustain it than to conjure it."

"But it's *your* essence," I pointed out. "Does it work to transfer it to someone else?"

Allie shrugged. "Never tried. Should we test it again?"

"I guess so." There wasn't an ounce of confidence in my voice.

Allie and I spent the better part of the afternoon in the valley trying to get *something* to appear in my hand. But nothing did.

My frustrations grew. How could Allie act like this was so easy? She wouldn't know what struggle was if it slapped her in the face.

Maybe she needs a slap in the face. The girl's too perfect for her own good.

After several hours, I thought I felt something out of the ordinary sizzle in my palm, but it only lasted a second. The next moment, voices coming from the top of the valley distracted me.

"Crap," Allie muttered.

I glanced toward the top of the staircase to see three figures headed our way. "What is it?"

Allie crossed her arms and pursed her lips. "It's trouble."

8

thin girl with long blond hair led the way down the stairs. Two muscular guys followed behind her. She laughed at something one of them said.

"I thought no one came here," I said to Allie.

Her expression contained a hint of disgust. "Only people from Galen High."

I could tell when the group spotted us because their laughter died down instantly.

"Uh, maybe we should go," I suggested. "We've been here long enough. They can have the valley to themselves."

I didn't need an audience.

"No way," Allie argued. "We were here first."

My eyes followed the group of three. The blonde held her head high and her back straight as if she owned the place. The two guys were good looking, even from this distance, but they almost looked *too* old to be in high school. It was like I'd stepped into some supernatural TV drama where all the actors were in their thirties even though they were supposed to be seventeen.

"Allie," I pleaded. "I haven't made any progress since we've been here. I don't think I'll start any time soon. Let's go."

Allie's shoulders dropped. "Yeah, okay. It's really not fun training around these guys anyway."

"You don't get along?"

That much was obvious.

She sighed. "They think they rule the school, but really the Saints are better than the Beasts."

"Saints? Beasts?"

"We train in groups," Allie explained. "Every group gets to choose their own team name. Marek, Kyle, and I train together with a couple others. Fletcher says the rivalry helps make us better."

I wanted to ask more questions about the inner workings of Galen High, but before I could, Blondie and her two bodyguards reached us.

"What's going on?" Blondie asked curiously. I half expected her to cross her arms and demand an answer.

"Uh, this is Ryn." Allie gestured to me. "She just moved here. She's starting at Galen this year."

Blondie tilted her head slightly. "I didn't know we were getting any new kids."

"It was a last minute thing," I told her vaguely.

"Welcome to Eagle Valley," she said with a smile. "I'm Casey. This is Troy and Trenton."

To my surprise, Casey held her hand out in my direction. I shook it, knowing I couldn't refuse.

"What school did you used to go to?" Casey asked casually.

"I've been to a couple—ow!"

A pain shot through my toe. I glanced over at Allie, wondering why she'd stomped on me. By the look on her face, she didn't want me to answer the question. When I glanced back at Casey, I realized she was asking which *Davina* school I'd been to. It was too late. Casey had already caught on.

"You mean you've never been to a Davina school before?" Her blond brows shot up.

"Well, uh… no, not exactly." I began to feel vulnerable. I certainly wasn't making a good first impression.

Except that Casey didn't make fun of me or throw a snide remark my way like I thought she might.

Instead, she simply smiled. "Don't feel bad. Trenton didn't show up until sophomore year, and he's going to be one of the best Protectors once we graduate. It's loads of fun. You just want to make sure you end up on a good team. Some can be *better* than others."

Her eyes darted toward Allie for a moment, who was desperately trying not to make eye contact.

I smiled back at her. "Thanks. I think I have a great team of people in mind already. Allie and I were just leaving. Have fun training."

I grabbed Allie's elbow and dragged her toward the stairs.

"She's really good, you know," Allie called back to Casey.

Casey crossed her arms and rolled her eyes. "If you mean by *your standards*, I feel sorry for her."

"Bite me," Allie called, but my grip dug deeper into her arm as we distanced ourselves from the group of three Davina. "Ryn has powers you wouldn't believe."

"Okay." Casey didn't sound convinced. "I'll believe that when I see it. Though, maybe your team could use the extra help."

Allie finally drew her attention away from Casey when we hit the stairs.

"What a *bitch*," she said under her breath. "She thinks they're so much better, but we get ratings based on how good we are. We totally crushed them last year."

"Allie," I tried, but she didn't respond between her complaints about Casey.

"Her team wouldn't be half as good without Troy and Trenton on it. I could totally take her one-on-one."

"Allie," I hissed again halfway up the stairs.

"What?"

"Why would you say that?"

She blinked several times. "Well, she *is* a bitch."

"No, not that. Why would you tell her I had amazing powers? I can't even conjure a basic fireball. Do you *want* her to have something else to ridicule you with?"

Allie and I reached the top of the steps and entered the trees before she spoke again.

"First of all, they're not fireballs. And besides, it's not like it's not true. Marek told me what happened the other night. I *wish* I was sober enough to have seen it. He said you were amazing."

"I didn't know what I was doing! I wasn't any better than he was. He knocked one of them out."

"Yeah, but you—" Allie's voice stopped dead.

"What?" I demanded.

"Oh, I'm sorry." Her tone grew soft. "They didn't tell you, did they?"

"Tell me what?"

Our pace slowed, but Allie moved ahead of me. A waterfall of black hair concealed her face. "I'm not sure I should be the one to tell you. I think Fletcher should."

"What's going on?" My voice rose.

I knew there was a lot left to learn, but I didn't like the idea of anyone omitting information. I thought being one of them meant I could trust them.

Allie brushed her fingers through her hair like she was uncomfortable. "I'm sure they didn't mean to keep it from you. Honestly, it's easy to forget how much you don't know. The rest of us grew up with this stuff. It's kind of common sense to us."

My skin heated. "Are you saying I'm stupid?"

"What?" Allie looked genuinely shocked. "No. Of course not. I just—I don't think I can explain it well enough."

We stepped out of the trees at the back of Galen High. Allie stopped and turned to me.

She spoke in a small voice. "I don't think it's something you should hear from me. Please trust me."

I sighed, feeling bad for how uncomfortable I made her. "We don't know each other that well yet, Allie, but I *do* trust you."

That doesn't mean I can't be mad at you.

We drove home in silence.

Allie turned to me when we pulled into her driveway. "You should stay the night."

"I can't." Not if she was going to keep secrets from me. "Mom's going to throw a big enough fit as it is about how we never spend time together."

"Maybe I should stay at your house, then," she suggested.

Sure. Just invite yourself over. How nice of you.

"I'd have to ask my mom," I said.

"You really shouldn't be alone, Ryn. Not with the demons out there."

I made a point to glance up and down our street. "I don't see any demons. I'll be fine, Allie. I'll see you tomorrow."

I opened the door and hurried across her lawn to my house. I started up the stairs to my room, but the sound of my name stopped me.

I peeked into the living room. "What?"

Mom sat on the couch crocheting her afghan. "Why didn't you finish your chores?"

Excuse me? I'd done the dishes and cleaned the bathroom and the living room. I'd even gone so far as to scrub the toilet and vacuum the carpets. Did she somehow know Allie had helped me?

"What do you mean?" I asked innocently. I *was* innocent.

"You have a pile of dirty laundry in the basement."

Oh, right. *That.*

"I'll get to it. I promise."

Just not now.

"Okay..." She didn't quite sound convinced, but she didn't push it.

I took it as an invitation to ignore her.

In my room, I plopped down on the bed and pulled out my phone. If Allie wasn't going to tell me the truth, I'd talk to someone who would.

Can we talk?

I stared down at my text on the screen. I'd texted Marek thirteen minutes ago, and he still hadn't responded. What kind of freak goes longer than ten minutes without texting someone back?

Maybe he was out riding his bike.

The phone shook in my hand. I contemplated sending him another text in case he hadn't seen the first notification, but I didn't want to seem desperate.

Except I was desperate.

Thirteen minutes turned into twenty. Twenty-three minutes after sending the first text, I began typing out a second message. Before I could finish and hit send, my phone chimed. Butterflies fluttered in my stomach.

Sorry, I'm busy.

My excitement quickly died. What could he possibly be doing? Modeling underwear?

I need to talk to you, I texted back.

His response came six minutes later. **No time.**

I stared at the screen and read his text at least five

times. Allie wasn't willing to talk to me, and Marek was busy. Did I have any other options?

Do you have Fletcher's number? I texted.

At least *he'd* tell me the truth.

Marek's next text came almost instantly. *Are you in trouble?*

No. Why would he think that? *I just have more questions.*

Sorry. He's busy, too.

My fingers pressed hard against the screen as I typed. *Doing what?*

He's with me.

Obviously, they couldn't both be modeling underwear. What were they up to?

We'll talk tomorrow, his text said. *Gotta go.*

Tomorrow seemed too far away.

9

By the way I screamed, you would've guessed I was being murdered. Over the roar of the wind, I didn't think even Marek could hear my screeching. We sped quickly down a secluded road near the edge of town the following afternoon. I wrapped my arms tightly around his torso.

"Slow down!" I cried, but I didn't think he heard me. I tried to peek over his shoulder to view the speedometer on his bike, but I didn't want to loosen my grip on his body. We had to be doing at least twenty miles per hour over the speed limit, and our speed was only increasing.

My screams turned into laughter. "Seriously, slow down," I called, but I sounded anything but serious.

Marek had said he wanted to show me something fun. I didn't think he meant *this*. I squeezed my eyes shut. For a moment, I could imagine myself flying.

Marek slowed the bike. I was surprised to find a wave of disappointment wash over me. He pulled over to the side of the road and twisted toward me. I forced myself to release him. Cool air rushed between us.

"Having fun yet?" he asked.

No matter how much I tried to suppress the smile on my face, it only grew wider. "I'm having more fun than I thought I would."

"Good."

"I thought you said earlier you were going to show me magic."

"No," Marek corrected. "I said I was going to show you something *like* magic."

I laughed. "That's not fair."

Marek smirked. "Oh, you thought the bike ride was it? No, this is just a warmup. What I'm going to show you is much, *much* more amazing."

Excitement sizzled in my bones. What could he possibly have in store?

"Ready for another go?" He winked before facing forward and revving the engine.

Before I knew it, we were back on the road again. I could've sworn Marek went even faster this time. Too soon, he slowed as we neared Galen High.

My knees shook when we stopped and dismounted the bike. I removed the helmet and shook my hair out.

"Are we going to the valley?" I asked in enthusiasm. "It was *so* pretty there when Allie took me."

Marek's smile widened, and that weakness returned to my knees. "We sure are. You ready?"

I nodded and eagerly followed behind him. "What are you going to show me?"

Marek threw back a knowing smile.

"You mean it's a surprise?"

His smile didn't fade. "You're going to love it."

"What is it?"

Marek ignored my question. "There's a lot to learn about Davina, and unfortunately, you freaked out before we could tell you much."

"I'm sorry. I must seem like a total foreigner."

Marek shrugged. "Don't feel bad. You're not the only Davina to grow up not knowing what they are."

I wanted to ask who he was talking about. Before I got a word out, we broke through the trees and into the clearing that opened to the valley.

The cloud cover had grown thicker since yesterday afternoon, casting a dull gray hue across the landscape. It looked like a storm was rolling in, but it didn't smell like rain.

Marek began stripping off his jacket without saying a word. Caught off guard, I remained silent.

"There are a few things you should know about Davina," he said as he tossed his jacket aside. "And this is one of them."

An involuntary intake of breath passed my lips as he pulled his t-shirt over his head. I knew it was rude to stare, but I couldn't tear my gaze from his torso. Marek flexed his upper body, accenting his six pack and his tan, toned arms. I was so mesmerized by him that I didn't take a moment to ask what he was doing. Surely he didn't mean to show me that all Davina were drop-dead gorgeous.

A moment later, I realized Marek wasn't showing me

his muscles at all. As he flexed, two white shapes rose behind him. They grew increasingly larger until I could finally make them out.

I gasped.

What looked like massive eagle wings had sprouted from his back. They were covered in silky white feathers and stretched wider than his arms. They were so beautiful; I wanted to reach out and touch them.

Without saying a word, Marek turned from me and took off sprinting toward the steep decline in front of us. His wings pulled into him for a moment. In a single leap, he hurled his body forward and spread his wings wide once again.

I stared in disbelief. Marek flapped his wings several times and then held them straight out parallel to the ground. He looked like the most majestic bird in the sky.

As soon as he began losing altitude, his wings pumped again to push himself higher. His body tilted to the left and circled around the empty field below us.

He began his flight back toward me. My body remained frozen at the top of the hill, completely mesmerized. Marek came so close to me that I thought he might land, but instead, he shifted course at the last second. Wind rushed by my face, and I beamed.

Marek locked his wings out, and they carried him on a graceful descent. Just when I thought he might touch the ground, he flapped his wings in one powerful, agile motion and shot straight into the air again.

I cheered and clapped in exhilaration.

Marek landed beside me. His massive wings flapped to slow his momentum, blowing my hair away from my face.

"Oh my God!" I managed to say. "No wonder people call you angels. I had no idea. Marek, they're beautiful."

Involuntarily, I reached a hand toward his outstretched wings. I thought better of it at the last second and jerked my fingers away.

"It's okay," he said kindly. "You can touch them."

My breath wavered as I inched closer to him. Carefully, I reached my hand out. My fingers connected with the soft, velvety feathers, and my breath hitched. Forget the fact that I'd just seen *wings* sprout out of Marek's back; what really got me was how soft and perfect his wings were. I couldn't wrap my head around the fact that they were real.

"But… how?" I asked, barely able to get the words out. "How do you do it?"

Marek shrugged, and his wings moved with him. "We just do. Think of it like shape shifting."

I ran my fingers down the feathers. "Are you saying Davina are like… shape shifting eagles?"

I caught Marek smile from out of the corner of my eye. It was the first time I managed to pull my gaze off his wings.

"Why do you think this place is called Eagle Valley?" he asked. Before I had a chance to answer, he spoke again. "No, we're not eagles. And before you say it again, we're not angels, either."

"I wasn't going to say that."

Marek rolled his eyes and pulled his wings into his

back. I retreated a step to give him space. The wings shrunk behind him until they vanished. A wave of disappointment washed over me; I wanted to stare at them longer.

"I wasn't thinking," he said. "I should've had you change before we came."

"What do you mean?"

"You want to fly, don't you?"

I drew in a breath of excitement. "You don't really think I can do that, do you?"

Marek furrowed his brow. "Of course I do. You're a Davina."

"Well, I didn't have much luck when Allie was trying to show me—"

"That's because Allie's never had to teach anyone before. Besides, the wings are easier. Let's start with that. But you'll have to change first. Most of the girls wear racerback tank tops. They won't get in the way of your wings. You have one, right?"

I nodded.

Marek turned to grab his t-shirt from the ground. For the first time, I got a look at his back. My gut instantly twisted.

Two raised scars ran along the length of his shoulder blades. It was as if his wings had sliced right through his skin… Except, the raised, discolored lines looked like they'd been trying to heal for years, not mere seconds.

He didn't notice me staring. "We'll go get it and then come back—"

"Marek." I spoke softly, but the shock in my tone got

him to look at me. "Are you hurt?" I stepped forward and ran my fingers across his back.

Marek shrugged me off and slipped his shirt on quickly. "No, it doesn't hurt."

"Does everyone get those scars?" My back heated as I imagined wings tearing through my flesh.

Marek bent again to scoop up his jacket. He stepped toward me and spoke quietly, like his words were meant only for me. "Everyone has scars, Ryn."

He was so close that his breath danced across my face.

"Am I going to get scars like that once I... you know?" My voice dropped to a whisper.

Marek started for the trees. For a moment, I thought maybe he didn't hear me.

"Not like this," he finally said.

I followed behind him. "Well, if everyone has them—"

"Not everyone has the same type of scars, Ryn. These are mine."

For every step he took, I had to take two. "What are they from, then?"

Marek whirled around so fast that I nearly rammed into him.

"Do you want me to show you how to fly or not?" he snapped.

I blinked in surprise. "I—I just wanted to prepare myself in case..."

"In case of what?" he asked sharply. "Nothing bad is going to happen to you." He sounded more irritated than reassuring.

I crossed my arms. "How can I be sure of that if I don't

know what gave you those scars? I don't know anything about this Davina stuff. What if I mess up?"

I thought I caught a hint of an eye-roll in Marek's expression.

"You're not going to mess up. Again, do you want to learn how to fly or not? Because we're just wasting time."

I stood my ground. "I'm not in a rush."

Marek sighed in annoyance and turned from me. Instead of heading down the path, he veered off into the trees in a straight shot toward his bike. "Whatever. If you're going to push it, maybe I don't *want* to teach you."

He muttered something else about respecting privacy, but I didn't hear the rest of it because this time I didn't follow him.

Watching him walk away caused a guilty sensation to settle in my gut. As soon as he disappeared through the thick brush, I felt like I might hurl.

"Marek, wait!" I called after him.

At that point, I wasn't sure he could hear me.

I hurried into the trees, intent on apologizing, but I had no way of knowing where exactly he went. I followed my best guess and continued toward where his motorcycle was parked. I still didn't catch a glance of him.

I increased my pace to try to catch up. Almost immediately, my foot caught a root, and my body lurched forward. On the descent, I caught a flash of a black object flying by my head.

It took a moment for me to realize what had happened. I snapped my head in the direction the essence came from.

My heart jumped at the sight of a cloaked figure stalking my way.

10

"Marek!" I cried as I scrambled to my feet. I told myself I should run, but I stood grounded by fear.

The demon let out the kind of laugh that sent a shiver down my spine.

"You're all alone now, Little Angel," he said.

I recognized his voice from the party on Friday night. *Dorian.*

My hands shook. "I thought your kind didn't come into Eagle Valley."

His face was shadowed under his hood, but I could sense the smirk in his voice. "Not usually, but I've made an exception for you."

A dark fireball formed in his hand. This time, I was prepared. As he hurled it my way, I dodged his attack and fell to the earth. I raised my dirt-covered palms and tried to conjure a fireball myself, but my hands remained empty.

The demon lunged for me. His body crashed into mine

and knocked me on my back. Almost immediately, he was on top of me, straddling me.

I managed to get my knees under him and forced him off of me. I rushed to my feet, but I was back on the ground a moment later. His cold fingers gripped my ankle. My foot connected with his face, but he only tightened his hold on me.

Before I knew it, he was on top of me again. He squeezed my wrists together tightly and held them above my head with one hand.

"Marek!" I tried to scream, but Dorian slapped his free hand over my mouth.

I lifted my hips to shove him off me, but it was no use. He was bigger and stronger, and I didn't know how to use my essence yet to defend myself. My legs thrashed against the ground, sending dry leaves flying.

"You're a fighter." Dorian sounded amused. "Should we get started now, then?" His ice cold hand slithered up my abdomen.

Nausea slammed into my gut.

"Marek!" I shrieked. Tears rose to my eyes, and my vision blurred.

Dorian's hand reached my breast, and he squeezed. I writhed beneath him, but there was nothing I could do to free myself.

"Please stop!" I sobbed.

He lowered his face to mine. I squeezed my eyes shut and twisted my face away from him.

His cool breath rushed across my ear. "You don't have to fight this. With you on my side, we could do anything."

His fingers moved to my waistline.

Oh, hells to the no.

"Screw you!" I did the only thing I could think of. I spit in his face.

Dorian recoiled like he couldn't believe what I'd done. His hand left my skin, and he reached beneath his hood to wipe the spit away.

"Bitch!" he roared.

His palm cracked across the side of my face, and I cried out in pain. The moment I expected another blow to come, Dorian's weight vanished.

When I opened my eyes, Marek was scrambling on the ground beside me. He rose to his knees above the demon and brought his fist down onto his face. I heard a crunch as the two connected.

Dorian's hood fell. His face was so pale and thin that he could easily be mistaken for a skeleton, and his black irises hinted at a darkness beyond human capacity.

I shuddered.

The blood streaming from Dorian's nose contained hints of red, but it was darker than I expected. It looked like someone had mixed black paint with the crimson liquid.

Marek shifted to wrap his arm around the demon's neck. Dorian flailed, struggling to breathe. His face darkened the more Marek squeezed.

"Stop it, Marek." My hands shook against the ground as I pushed myself to my feet. The left side of my face still stung.

Marek only squeezed Dorian harder.

"You're going to kill him!" I shouted.

"*He* was going to kill *you!*" Marek roared without loosening his grip.

"I don't care," I cried. "It's not right!"

"This is what we do, Ryn. This is a war. Don't you realize that?"

It didn't matter. I couldn't watch him do this.

"You can't fight evil with evil," I protested. "There has to be another way."

Marek hesitated for only a second, but it was enough for Dorian to gain the upper hand and slip out of his grasp.

Dorian balled his hand into a fist and smashed it into the side of Marek's face. Marek stumbled to the side. I let out a screech in surprise. Before either of us could fight back, Dorian raced away into the forest.

I rushed to Marek's side and dropped to my knees beside him. "Are you okay?"

Marek glared at me and wiped the blood from his lip. "You're going to regret that, Ryn. He's going to come after you again."

Tears welled in my eyes, but I remained silent.

Marek stood and reached out a hand to me. "Let's get out of here."

11

My heart hammered, and it didn't stop all the way home.

As soon as Marek parked in front of my house, I pulled the helmet off and shoved it his way. I couldn't bring myself to go inside. Instead, I paced back and forth on the sidewalk next to him. He opened his mouth to say something but closed it again. The silence was agonizing.

"What?" I snapped.

Marek recoiled.

"Clearly you have something to say," I accused.

"I…" He trailed off.

"Are you hiding something from me? Just say it."

Marek sighed. "I'm not trying to *hide* anything from you. We just didn't think he'd attack, not when…"

My brows shot up. "Not when, what? What aren't you telling me?"

Marek wouldn't look at me. "I shouldn't have left you alone. Not even for a second."

"I'm alone all the time," I pointed out.

"Not recently." Marek finally lifted his gaze to meet mine. "I was going to say… we didn't think he'd attack when one of us was nearby… protecting you."

I froze. "What are you saying? You've been stalking me?"

Marek's eyebrow twitched. "Well, that just makes it sound creepy. We've been keeping an eye on you."

"Who's *we*?" I demanded.

"Me, Allie, Fletcher. Kyle took a shift last night watching your house."

I gritted my teeth. "You didn't have to do that."

Marek climbed off his bike. "We did. Clearly you can't defend yourself."

He had me there.

"What did you expect to happen?" he asked rhetorically. "I said he'd be back, or don't you remember?"

"I—" I went silent.

I remembered his words from Friday night. For some reason, I hadn't processed them at the time.

"I don't know what I thought," I admitted. "Frankly, I was sure I was going crazy."

Marek stepped toward me slowly, as if testing to make sure I wasn't going to run away from him. "We *were* going to tell you everything, but then even the basics overwhelmed you. We thought it was best to show you a little at a time rather than dumping everything on you all at once. Honestly, I thought you might run away and get yourself killed."

"I have no plans of getting myself killed."

Marek raised an eyebrow and took another cautious step forward. "And running away?"

I sighed and threw my hands in the air. "Well, sure, it might be something worth considering. I don't know if I can actually trust you people. I don't know if any of this is even *real*. I don't know if—"

Marek grabbed my wrists, but I jerked away immediately.

"Don't touch me," I bit harshly.

"Calm down, Ryn," he said in a soothing voice.

Marek reached out for me again. I wedged my arms between our chests and pushed away. I had no desire to be touched right now, not after what happened.

"Stop trying to comfort me," I said with an edge to my tone. "I barely even know you."

"But you trust me, don't you?" he asked softly.

It took me several moments to ponder the question. He *had* saved me from the demons twice now. That had to count for something. And I had no reason to believe he was lying about anything he'd told me so far.

I searched his eyes for signs of dishonesty. I couldn't find any.

"I don't know," I finally said in a whisper. "I don't think I have a choice."

"Please let me help you," he said softly.

This time, I came to him. I allowed him to wrap me in his arms. Marek was nothing like Dorian. His embrace was warm and comforting, a sanctuary in stark contrast to Dorian's icy cold touch. I let myself melt into Marek's chest, and I inhaled the scent of his leather jacket.

"You can trust me," he whispered.

I swallowed the lump in my throat. "Am I going to be safe, Marek?"

He paused for a beat. "Demons won't come this far into town. And during the school year, there are a lot more Davina coming and going from the valley. That place is usually pretty safe, too."

"Usually?" I asked warily.

"Well, it's not every day you offend a demon and become a target. They don't usually try to mess with us like that."

"You're using that word a lot."

"What word?"

"*Usually*. Why would he be after me? Why not you? You were the one who hurt him the other day."

"Oh, um…"

"You're doing it again," I accused, pulling away from him. "You're hiding something from me. What is it you don't want to tell me?"

Marek dropped his gaze. "I thought you understood."

"Understood what? Marek, just tell me."

He finally looked at me. "Ryn… you killed his friend. He's out for revenge. And he won't stop until he kills you."

12

I drew in a sharp breath.

"No," I insisted. "No way. I would *never*."

It didn't matter that Marek had just pointed out that my life was in danger. All I could focus on was the fact that I'd killed someone.

"You didn't know what you were doing. It was an accident." He said it like that justified what I'd done.

Suddenly, I felt like I couldn't breathe. I grabbed onto his shoulders to steady myself. My fingers dug into his leather jacket.

After deciding I wasn't going to puke, I relaxed my grip and drew away from him.

"You really had no idea?" Marek asked curiously.

"That I killed someone? Yeah, because that happens every day." My face grew hot.

"He vanished in a puff of smoke," Marek pointed out. "What did you think happened to him?"

"I don't know! I've spent my entire life thinking the demons were in my head. I thought I was hallucinating."

That's what everyone told me the last time something like this happened.

"He could've teleported or something," I said. "It'd make just as much sense as the rest of this. Besides, you used the same thing on the other guy, and he got right back up and is apparently doing fine."

"It's not—Ryn, calm down."

I covered my face with my hands, still unable to believe it. "Why'd he disappear like that?"

What kind of fantasy world had I fallen into?

"It has something to do with the demon's curse," Marek explained. "They live on a different plane of existence. Without their life force tethering them here, their bodies fall into a plane we don't have access to."

I shuddered at the thought of demon bodies piled up throughout the world, rotting away on another plane of existence we couldn't see. It quite literally sounded like Hell.

"It's not a bad thing," Marek assured me. "He was just a demon."

"Just a demon?" I balled my hands into fists and paced away from him several steps. "That doesn't change the fact that I *killed* him."

"That's what Davina *do*, Ryn. We help protect the world from demons."

"Then why are there so many of them still running around?" I couldn't help the accusation from slipping out.

"Believe it or not, they're actually not that easy to kill.

We can't just shoot them." He paused momentarily. "It's complicated."

"I have all day," I challenged.

Marek sighed. "What do you want, Ryn?"

I closed my eyes and attempted to steady my breath. There were so many answers to that question. I wanted to erase the last hour of my life. I wanted to escape all of this, to live in a world where I never saw the demons and never learned I was a Davina. At the same time, I wanted to learn what I was capable of. I wanted to be able to defend myself.

"I want to see Fletcher," I said in a small voice.

Marek nodded. "Okay, we'll go see Fletcher. I'll give him a call." He pulled his phone from his pocket.

Just as he placed it to his ear and the other line began ringing, a familiar voice called from behind me.

"Hey." Allie crossed her lawn toward us.

Kyle followed behind her.

"What's going on?" Allie stopped beside me and glanced between us. "Is something wrong?"

How did I even begin to answer that question?

"Hey," Kyle said cheerfully. He lightly elbowed me in the side. "Don't look so glum. Cheer up."

I glared at him.

I noticed Marek subtly shake his head at Kyle out of the corner of my eye. Kyle's expression instantly fell.

"Hey, Fletcher," Marek said into the phone.

"What happened?" Allie asked me, her tone full of concern.

I looked up to the overcast sky then down at the sidewalk. Anything not to meet her gaze.

"We're meeting up with Fletcher," I told her like it explained everything. I didn't think I'd ever be able to truly explain it.

"The school?" Marek's voice came into focus again.

My head instantly snapped in his direction. "No!"

He furrowed his brow at me as he listened to Fletcher on the other end of the line.

"I don't want to go back there," I whispered.

Marek nodded in understanding. "Forget the school," he interrupted Fletcher. "We'll meet at your house."

"What's going on?" Allie demanded as soon as Marek hung up.

A muscle popped in Marek's jaw. "The demon found her. We're going to see Fletcher."

"We're coming with," Kyle insisted.

"Yeah," Allie agreed. "You two go together. Kyle and I will take my car."

"I'll come with you, too," I suggested.

"No," Allie insisted, pushing me toward Marek's motorcycle.

He was already sitting on it and holding the helmet out toward me.

I huffed. Now was not the time for Allie to play matchmaker. But I didn't want to waste the time arguing. I grabbed the helmet and put it on. I wrapped myself around Marek again, and we sped down the street.

We pulled up in front of a small ranch-style home at the end of a cul-de-sac. It was a simple one-story house with gray siding and stone accents. Two well-kept flowerbeds lined the edge of the house, and a carved wooden bear stood next to the front door with a welcome sign in his hands.

Marek placed a hand on my back as we approached the house.

Fletcher opened the front door for us before we even had a chance to knock. He wore tan slacks and a white button down shirt.

It wasn't until we were inside that I realized I was still wearing Marek's motorcycle helmet. I pulled it off and breathed in a deep breath. The house smelled like dryer sheets and freshly baked bread. It's what I thought my grandparents' house might smell like—if I'd ever met them.

"Sit down," Fletcher said, gesturing to the couch.

I set the helmet on the coffee table and sank into the couch cushions. Fletcher's living room was small, housing only a couch, recliner, and TV. Several photographs hung on the walls, but they were just to add a pop of color to the space; I didn't see any pictures of his family. The room was bathed in earthy tones. That, coupled with the smells I detected earlier, gave it a welcoming, homey ambiance.

I felt safe here.

Allie and Kyle entered a moment later. Allie sat beside me, and Kyle leaned against the arm of the couch next to her. Marek took my other side, and Fletcher sat in the recliner.

Fletcher fixed a serious expression on his face. "Tell me what happened."

My gut twisted. I didn't know if I could. I exchanged a wary glance with Marek. He took charge and began to recount the details from earlier. My hands shook against my knees when he told them how he'd returned to find Dorian attacking me. I was grateful he didn't go into detail. I could still feel Dorian's hand cupping my breast. The last thing I wanted to do was relive that moment.

The more Marek talked, the angrier he became. He rose from the couch and began pacing back and forth across the living room.

"I made a mistake," he said. "I had the chance to kill him, and I didn't."

"Calm down, James," Fletcher insisted.

Marek glared at him. "We should go back out there and hunt him down."

Kyle scoffed. "Yeah, because that worked so well the last time."

I instantly became alert. "What do you mean?"

Marek stopped pacing and raked his fingers through his hair. "He's talking about last night. Fletcher, Kyle, and I were out there trying to hunt this guy down."

So that's what he'd been busy doing when I texted him.

"He knew we were on his tail, though," Marek said. "We never got close enough to him. I was hoping we'd scared him off, but…"

Tension formed in my head. "You still don't have to kill him."

"Would you rather he kill you first?" Marek's voice rose.

"Calm down," Fletcher repeated. "Sit, James."

Marek's chest rose and fell rapidly, and his lips pressed into a thin line. After several moments, he finally gave in and sat next to me.

Nobody spoke for several seconds.

I was the first to break the silence. "I don't think he was trying to kill me, Marek. He was trying to…" I couldn't finish the sentence.

"He was having fun with you," Marek said with disgust. "He would've killed you as soon as he was done."

Nausea returned, and a lump rose in my throat. "That doesn't make killing him okay."

I had to believe Marek was better than that.

"What do you suggest?" Marek snapped. "It's not like there's a prison we can lock him up in."

"He has a point," Kyle said.

"Everybody needs to calm down," Fletcher said in a commanding voice.

The four of us stared back at him.

"Ryn," Fletcher said softly, "are you okay?"

My shoulders relaxed. I appreciated that he cared.

"I'm scared," I admitted. "But I'm okay for now."

Fletcher's gaze dropped. "There's something you should know."

Oh, crap. I had no idea what to expect. I couldn't even manage to come up with insane possibilities in my head.

"I'm not going anywhere," I stated. I just hoped I meant it after I heard what he had to say.

"Good," he said. "Because if you did, the entire human race would be put in jeopardy."

I forced my shock down so it couldn't overwhelm me. I could hear it in Fletcher's voice. There was something bigger going on here, bigger than the age-old war he'd mentioned before.

And somehow, I had something to do with it.

13

"What—what do you mean?" My voice wavered.

Fletcher leaned forward. "We believe you have the Power of Grace."

I glanced around the room, hoping someone would elaborate without me having to ask.

Thankfully, Fletcher continued. "Marek knew when he met you. It's evidenced in the color of your essence—purple. Most Davina can only conjure white essence. Yours, Ryn, is special."

This must be what Allie wouldn't tell me about before.

"What does it mean?" My hands shook slightly as I thought about what I'd done with it. "It's more powerful?"

"Yes. Most Davina can't kill with their essence—only stun," Fletcher explained. "We have to turn to other means or use weapons to kill the Aedes, the same way they do with us."

"Other weapons?" I asked cautiously.

91

"I told you the Aedes' curse doesn't apply to materials that originate from another realm," Fletcher said. "When the Davina first returned here, they brought certain things from their realm back with them. We have a small collection of what we call Davina Blades. They're daggers that came from Vehena. We can use those against the Aedes. You, Ryn, are another type of weapon."

My body gave an involuntary shudder at the word *weapon*.

"Your essence is unique," Fletcher said.

I crossed my arms. I tried to remain as calm as I could, but my words came out flat and accusatory. "Because I can kill. What if I don't want to?"

Allie placed a comforting hand on my shoulder. Her eyes pleaded with me to hear Fletcher out before jumping to conclusions.

I uncrossed my arms.

"There's more you should know about our history," Fletcher said. "When the Davina created humans, the Aedes believed it to be a form of trickery. They thought the Davina created humans in an attempt to build an army faster and to force the Aedes back to Malum. They felt betrayed; they'd once again been cast aside by those who were more powerful than they were. The Aedes soon realized, however, that humans were powerless, and they became power-hungry. They were finally stronger than someone else, and they exploited that."

I considered this for a moment. "Allie said they feed off human essence."

"Yes," Fletcher confirmed.

"But humans don't have essence," I stated.

Fletcher's forehead creased. "Of course they do. Remember what I told you. Essence is the energy that makes up who you are as a person. Humans simply can't access their essence physically like we can. The Aedes, however, found a way to tap in to it. It's essentially an unlimited power source. But that doesn't mean it can be stolen without consequences. When an Aedes feeds off a human's essence, it throws the balance of their four energies off. Humans can easily be manipulated then. Many will go into deep depressions as long as their essence is being fed upon. Others will be overcome with greed or jealousy, all the things that make the Aedes themselves evil. The Aedes do it for amusement."

I trembled. Fletcher's story brought back too many horrible memories. And now those memories were starting to make sense.

"How do I fit in to that?" I asked.

"Because of the way the Aedes treated the humans, the Davina became protective," Fletcher continued. "That's what started the second war, the one we're still fighting today. The Davina believed the earth belonged to the humans. They forced the Aedes back to Malum and sealed off the portals to that realm. They decided to seal off their own portals to Vehena as well to prevent any of their own kind from exploiting the humans.

"Sixteen original Davina stayed behind to seal the portals. Afterward, they found their power so drained they'd nearly given up their immortality. Remember that the Divinities tried sealing off Malum before only for the gateways to reopen?"

I nodded.

"The Davina knew it could happen again. The realms touch and can't be broken apart. They made a difficult decision. At the time, their work was finished, but they feared what might happen if another war broke out and they weren't around to help. They decided to freeze their bodies in time by sending their consciousness and essence into the earth, where it would be safe until they made their return. As legend tells it, their essence would return if we had to call upon the Originals once again for protection."

I couldn't believe what I was hearing. It all sounded like make-believe, but Fletcher told it like it was fact, history.

"What does that have to do with me?" I asked.

Fletcher took a deep breath. "Your power is a sign that we're in danger. If the Power of Grace has returned, it means the line between the realms is thinning. The problem is that we don't know where to find the portal that poses the threat. Even if we could find it, we'd need an Original's power to close it. This is why the Power of Grace is important."

The room went silent for a beat.

"Grace was among one of the Originals," Fletcher explained, "and she's our last hope."

Was Fletcher out of his mind? He didn't actually think I played a role in this, did he?

"So," I said, "I have some other Davina's power inside of me?"

Allie and Fletcher nodded in unison.

"What am I supposed to do with it?" I wasn't sure I wanted the answer.

"It's your job to wake Grace." Fletcher said it like it was so simple.

"Excuse me?" My eyes must've widened to twice their size.

Fletcher frowned. "I apologize if I'm not explaining it well enough."

"I get it," I said. "It's just a lot to take in."

Fletcher nodded in agreement and then continued. "A group of Aedes managed to stay behind when the portals were sealed. When they heard about what the Originals had done, they turned to hunting them down so they could never awaken and use their powers again."

I drew in a sharp breath. "Why would they do that?"

Fletcher shook his head like he'd never quite understand. "Same reason they want to kill the rest of us. Power. If we're not around to stop them, they can play their games with the humans and manipulate them like puppets. They've never been in a position of power before; this would put them there."

Marek cut in. "Not to mention that if we don't have the power of the Originals, we'd never be able to seal off the portals to Malum again."

I stared at him in confusion. "Why is that a bad thing, though?"

"Have you seen the world today?" Marek asked rhetorically. "The demons have bred and grown their numbers so much that things are bad enough as it is. They're the ones corrupting the world. If the portal opens, the rest of the

Aedes get through. Their numbers skyrocket; they kill us off; and they manipulate the humans to extinction. It's how they get revenge for their ancestors."

I looked between Fletcher and Marek, still trying to absorb all this information. "Do you really believe all this?"

Everyone nodded in unison.

"So, if the demons hunted the Originals, where are they today?" I asked.

Fletcher sighed. "When it started, the Davina formed a secret society called Praesid dedicated to the protection of the Originals. They thought it was best to split the Originals up, and so members of Praesid moved the Originals across the globe. Every few centuries or so, they'd move again to keep anyone from tracking them down. Unfortunately, the Aedes managed to hunt down fifteen of the sixteen Originals and destroy their bodies with the help of humans through manipulation if needed."

"I thought you said the Originals were immortal," I pointed out.

Fletcher nodded. "In a sense. They didn't age, and they had incredible healing abilities, so they didn't die natural deaths. But that didn't mean they couldn't be destroyed. When the Originals sent their essence into their earth, their life force remained intact, which meant all four energies survived. They were only temporarily separated. When the Aedes destroyed their bodies, it severed their life force. Their consciousness ceased to exist, and their essence mixed with that of their ancestors to be recycled by later generations."

I dropped my head and pressed my fingers to my eyes.

This was all too much to take in. How could *I* possibly have anything to do with this?

I took a deep breath. "So they killed fifteen of the sixteen, which means Grace is the only one left."

"Yes," Fletcher confirmed.

"And she needs me to bring her back to life?"

"She's still alive," Fletcher said. "Her body is essentially frozen. By awakening her, you can restore her essence, and she can close the portal."

I glanced around the room in disbelief. Four pairs of eyes stared back at me, but nobody said a thing.

"Even if I was capable of something like this, I'd never know where to find her," I said. "Anyone else have any clues?"

I didn't expect an answer.

"Grace was lost over a century ago," Fletcher said. "Some believe her body was destroyed along with the others. Your power is evidence that she's still out there somewhere."

My mouth grew dry. "How—what—?" *Why me?* "You really think so?"

A smile crept across Fletcher's face. "Yes. I believe that Grace is somewhere in Eagle Valley."

I inhaled an audible breath. Even Allie made a noise beside me like this was news to her, too.

"Our town was settled over a hundred and fifty years ago by a group of Davina," Fletcher said. "It's very possible that they were part of Praesid. They would've brought her here and hidden her during settlement. And since there are so many of us here, she would've always been protected by default."

"But you're not the only town of Davina, are you?" I asked.

"Of course not," Allie said.

"No, no," Fletcher answered at the same time. "It's not the Davina population that made me think that Grace might be here. It's the fact that you showed up, Ryn. I think you might've been brought here for a reason."

My jaw dropped. "You're talking about fate?"

Fletcher shrugged. "In a sense, yes. I think you're here because Grace led you here."

I had to sit silent for a moment to let all of this sink in.

"Why didn't you mention this before?" I asked calmly, though my heart hammered. I guess I never gave him a chance.

"I was afraid it would all be too overwhelming for you," Fletcher admitted. "I've seen how some students react when we throw too much information on them at once."

He and Marek exchanged a glance, like they both knew exactly which student he was talking about. Neither of them cared to elaborate.

"How do you expect me to find her?" I asked.

Fletcher shifted in his chair. "I'm not sure I have an exact answer. You were chosen by Grace. Her magic will lead you to her."

Suddenly, Eagle Valley didn't seem so small anymore. I couldn't believe what he was asking me to do. Someone like Allie who had been exposed to this her whole life should have the Power of Grace, not me.

"What if I can't?" I challenged. "I have no idea what I'm doing."

"We'll figure it out," Fletcher assured me. "You'll be training with Marek, Allie, and Kyle. They're the best in their class. I'm sure you'll catch on quickly."

"And Fletcher is the best mentor in school," Allie said.

Fletcher shot her a smile. "Ryn, you're not alone. We'll teach you how to use your essence. We'll be here to help in any capacity we can. In the meantime, however, I would like you to train in private. I think it's best if no one knows you have the Power of Grace. If word gets out, it may not be long before the Aedes find out and realize, as I have, that Grace might be here in town. Then Eagle Valley would really have a war on their hands. Let's keep this between us five."

"But what about the demon that's after me?" I asked. "Doesn't he realize I'm different? Won't he tell?"

Fletcher took a long moment to breathe. "The recent incident is personal to him. He'll want to finish you off himself."

I didn't like how casually he said the words *finish you off*.

"I've been in touch with other Davina in town," Fletcher said. "We have a group of people looking for him. Obviously, we haven't caught him yet, which is why I want you with one of us at all times. If you stick by us, you won't have to worry. We'll take care of him."

The tension in my head intensified. I pressed my fingers to my temples.

"I can see we've overwhelmed you with information once again," Fletcher said in a regrettable tone.

"No, it's fine," I lied, still rubbing my head. "I had to know all of this anyway."

"Why don't you return home and think about it?" he suggested.

I nodded, not really looking at him even though my eyes were on his.

"Once you're ready, we'll get started on your training." He smiled. "The first step, after all, is teaching you how to use your powers. I believe as you become more in tune with them, you'll have a better sense of your connection with Grace. We'll discuss the next steps once you have a firm grasp on your essence."

I nodded when all I really wanted to do was shake my head and refuse. I wasn't equipped to handle all of this.

And I definitely wasn't interested in being the *chosen one* Fletcher thought I was.

14

arek stood. "Come on, Ryn. I'll drive you home."

I grabbed the motorcycle helmet from the coffee table and followed behind him. I walked slowly, still trying to make sense of everything Fletcher had told me.

Outside, Allie and Kyle waved goodbye to us and climbed into her car.

Marek swung his leg over the seat of his bike, but I didn't make a move to climb on. I stared down at the helmet in my hands.

"What's wrong?" Marek sounded genuinely concerned.

Everything.

"Life is never going to be the same again, is it?" I whispered.

Marek's shoulders dropped. "No, it's not."

"I guess that means I'll never be normal." Not that I ever was.

Marek laughed lightly. "Where's the fun in being normal?"

I shrugged.

Marek quickly became serious. "Is there anything I can do to help? If you get on, I'll take you home."

Home. I wondered what that was like. Mom and I moved so much that nowhere ever really felt like home.

"I don't want to go home," I heard myself say.

"What do you want?" he asked kindly.

I finally looked at him, but I didn't answer. The truth was, I didn't know what I wanted.

A long silence stretched between us.

Finally, a small smile crept across his face. "Get on."

"Where are we going?" I asked.

"You want to be normal. Let's forget about all this stuff. Let's do something normal." His smile widened.

I couldn't help but smile back, even though that smile was filled with uncertainty. I placed the helmet on my head and climbed on the bike behind him.

"Do I even dare ask where we're going?" I shouted as the engine roared to life.

"You mean you don't like surprises?"

The bike lurched forward before I had a chance to answer.

Lately, surprises had been nothing but bad news, but I could tell by how excited he seemed that this one would be good.

~

Marek pulled into a driveway next to a two-story house. It looked a lot like our rental with the same big front porch, but there were clear differences. The brown vinyl siding made this house look a lot newer than ours, and the two-car garage had a basketball hoop attached to the front.

Marek cut the engine, and we both climbed off the bike.

"Do you play?" I asked, gesturing to the basketball hoop.

"Yeah, whenever Kyle comes over."

I handed Marek the helmet, and he tucked it under his arm.

Marek headed to the back door and led me inside a mud room. He placed the helmet on a small bench and hung his jacket up on a hook above it.

"James?" a high-pitched voice called from the next room.

I stepped into the kitchen behind Marek. A young girl who looked around eight stood on a chair at the counter and dug through one of the cabinets. She wore a red apron that was far too big on her.

"What is it, Piglet?" Marek playfully tugged at one of the ringlets in her pigtail.

She slapped his fingers away but smiled. "Me and Mom are making cookies."

"Mom and *I*," Marek corrected her.

She stuck her tongue out at him. "Mom and *I*. Want to help?"

"Not right now." Marek exchanged a glance with me.

The girl noticed me in the doorway for the first time.

"Ooh," she teased. "Is she your girlfriend?"

I had to refrain from bursting into laughter.

"No, Bailey," Marek answered. "She's just a friend."

Bailey set a bag of flour on the counter and hopped down from her chair. She eyed me curiously. "What's your name?"

I smiled at her. She was adorable.

"My name's Ryn."

She tilted her head. "That's an interesting name."

"It's short for Kathryn," I explained.

"I thought Kathy was short for Kathryn."

"Kathy makes me sound old," I told her. "I like Ryn better."

I'd been around Bailey's age when I chose the nickname for myself. It was the first time Mom and I moved. Mom called it our fresh start, and I took those words to heart. I told everyone at my new school to call me Ryn, and the name had stuck with me ever since.

Bailey looked up at me with bright eyes. "Do *you* want to make cookies with us?"

Cookies sounded delicious.

"No, Piglet," Marek answered for me.

"Actually, I love baking," I said. "Or did you have something else in mind?"

Marek's gaze shifted between mine and Bailey's. "Okay, Piglet. What kind are we making?"

Bailey jumped up and down in excitement. "Sugar cookies. You get the cookie cutters out." Her voice rose to call down the hall. "Mom! James brought his girlfriend over. They're going to help me make cookies."

A middle-aged woman entered the kitchen a moment

later. She looked exactly like Bailey minus the pigtails. Her eyes brightened curiously when she saw me.

"You didn't tell me you had a girlfriend," she said with a smile.

"She's not my girlfriend," Marek objected.

At least he didn't sound offended by it.

The woman crossed the kitchen and stuck her hand out toward me. "Hi, I'm Faith."

"Ryn," I introduced, shaking her hand.

"Well, Ryn," Faith said. "Welcome to our home."

All I heard her say was *welcome home.*

Marek and I spent the next several hours in the kitchen with Bailey baking and decorating cookies.

Marek swiped his finger across the inside of the bowl before I added the flour. He stuck his finger in his mouth and sucked the cookie dough from it.

"Get out of here." I swatted at him with my dirty spatula.

Marek's eyes widened innocently. "It's *my* kitchen."

I added the flour and started up the mixer. "You're throwing off the recipe."

"You're just going to eat the dough anyway," he pointed out.

I turned to Bailey, who was putting the flour away for me. "Help a girl out, would ya, Bailey?"

She hopped down from her chair and pushed at Marek. "If you're not gunna help, get out of the kitchen."

Marek laughed as she tried to push him out of the room. "I'm helping eat the cookies."

"You're ruining them," she complained.

I turned off the mixer.

Marek skirted around Bailey. "Look, they're done! I can eat them now."

Marek was closing in on me fast. I didn't know what came over me. I made the split second decision to scoop my finger into the bowl and fling a bit of dough at him. It hit him square between the eyes and bounced off his forehead.

He caught it with one hand and stopped a step away from me. His eyebrows rose in my direction.

"Nice shot," he said before popping the dough in his mouth.

Eventually, Bailey ate so many cookies that she began to complain about a stomach ache.

Marek encouraged her to relax on the couch, and he put a movie in for her.

I noticed it was starting to get dark outside, but I wasn't prepared to leave yet.

"Your sister's cute," I said when he returned to the kitchen. I nibbled on a heart-shaped cookie.

He leaned against the counter. "She's not my sister. She's my cousin."

"Oh," I said in surprise. "So, Faith isn't your mom?"

He shook his head and then swallowed a bite of cookie. "My aunt."

Marek didn't bother elaborating, and I didn't want to

push him to tell me about his family situation. I had a feeling it wasn't a fun story.

"What do you do when you aren't making cookies?" I asked.

Marek shrugged.

"All you do is play basketball and ride your bike?"

"No," he said defensively. "The bike's just for transportation, anyway."

"So you're *not* a badass biker dude?" I teased.

He laughed. "I never said I wasn't badass. As for a biker dude? I only bought the bike because my uncle's friend was selling it. It was cheaper than buying a car. I'd already been saving up from three summers of bailing hay and even more winters shoveling snow. I was sick of waiting for my own ride."

Marek motioned for me to follow him. He led me down a flight of stairs, and we entered an unfinished basement with cinderblock walls and a concrete floor. Exercise equipment lined one wall, and a TV stood against the other.

"This is basically what I do outside of school." He motioned to the exercise equipment.

Weightlifting definitely explained his abs.

I eyed a dumbbell on the floor. Maybe I needed to pick up weightlifting. I'd never understood the appeal before, but if I were stronger, I could defend myself better.

"Is it fun?" I asked.

Marek shrugged. "I don't do it because it's fun."

I sat at the bench press. "Why do you do it, then?"

"Training," he said simply.

"To become a Protector?" I already knew the answer.

Marek sat beside me on the bench. "Yeah."

Was I the only Davina who wasn't interested in fighting?

"Allie told me most Davina become Protectors," I said.

Marek nodded. "Yeah, but I'd do it even if it weren't so highly encouraged."

I looked at him curiously. "Why?"

Marek took a deep breath. "Because there's enough evil in the world already. If I can help get rid of some of it, then it'll be worth it."

He sounded so noble.

I tucked a strand of hair behind my ear. "You'll be good at it. The way you protected me earlier... I never said thank you."

He leaned in closer and spoke softly. "You didn't have to."

My breath hitched. He was so close to me. Close enough to kiss.

"Yes, I do," I whispered. "Thank you for everything."

He leaned even closer. My pulse quickened.

"Everything?" he asked like he didn't know what I meant.

"For earlier today..." I couldn't bring myself to talk about it. My skin crawled at the memory. "And for bringing me to meet your family. It made me feel normal. For a few hours, at least."

He gave a half-hearted smile. "I figured you could use a break."

And now I had to face reality again.

I dropped my gaze.

"What?" He pulled away slightly.

I shrugged. "There's just so much information, and there's still so much I don't know."

Marek shifted to straddle the bench facing me. "What do you want to know?"

I didn't have to think about it. "What are demons capable of? How much can they hurt us?"

"Their essence can stun you, but in case you didn't notice before, they have other means of hurting us."

"You mean strangling us to death?"

The image of the demon strangling Marek the night I met him flashed across my vision. My throat began to close up.

"Yeah," he said quietly. "They're pure evil."

I shook my head in disbelief. "That's horrible."

"They grow up in a different world than we do, quite literally."

I went silent for a beat. "Grow up? Like, there are baby demons?"

Marek laughed. "Well, are there baby Davina?"

"Um, yeah…" I said like it was obvious.

"The demons aren't immortal. The Divinities stole that from them. They have to reproduce the same way we do."

I'd never thought of that.

"Are they more powerful than we are?" I asked.

Marek shook his head. "The original Davina were a lot more powerful than the demons. But now our powers have been diluted by our human blood. The more time passes, the more magic we lose while theirs stays the same it's always been through every generation. Now we're closer to equals."

"That's what makes this war so dangerous?"

Marek nodded. "They used to be easier to defeat. The only way we've been able to grow our numbers is breeding with humans, but the power gets diluted every generation. Now the demons outnumber us. You see, not everyone with Davina blood develops full Davina powers."

I bit my bottom lip.

"I didn't mean you, Ryn. I saw what you can do. You're a Davina through and through."

"Then why is it so hard for me to conjure essence? You do it so effortlessly."

"Believe me, it wasn't always so easy." Marek reached out and forced my chin toward him.

I didn't resist.

He held my gaze intensely, never dropping his fingers from the side of my face. "You're doing amazing so far. I mean it."

I stared into his mesmerizing blue eyes, trying to convince myself he was telling the truth.

Marek shifted forward on the bench until we were just inches apart. It would be so easy to lean over and kiss him.

My phone buzzed in my back pocket, and we instantly jumped apart. I sighed and stood. It was my mother.

Where are you?

Hanging out with friends, I texted back. Just like I'd told her earlier.

It's getting late. Which was code for *I want you home right now*. Probably so I could cook her dinner.

I'll be home soon.

I turned back to Marek, who looked at me curiously. "Sorry. My mom wants me home. I should go."

Marek stood abruptly. "Let me drive you."

"No—" I started to say, but I cut off. I didn't want to walk home alone in the dark. "Okay, but on one condition."

"What's that?" he asked.

I smirked playfully. "Drive slow this time."

15

We pulled up in front of my house too soon. I wanted to hold onto him longer.

I was surprised when Marek walked me to the door. I turned to him with my hand on the doorknob. The porch light illuminated his features. His eyes danced across my face, and his lips curled into a hint of a smile.

I hardly knew Marek, and already I had this urge to give him a hug goodbye. After everything he'd done for me, I felt like he at least deserved that much.

"What?" he asked curiously.

I wasn't bold enough to hug him first.

"I still have so many questions." It was only an excuse to keep him here longer.

"Like what?" he asked.

He reached out a hand to tuck a strand of stray hair behind my ear. My skin heated where he'd touched me. It didn't even seem like he noticed what he'd done.

I dropped my hand from the doorknob. I'd much rather

stay out here talking to Marek than go inside. I didn't want him to leave.

"I don't know. Is there more I *should* know? Besides the fireballs and flying, what else can we do?"

"We can heal," he said. "Ever been sick, Ryn?"

"No," I answered automatically. The reality of it hit me so hard it nearly took my breath away. I sank into the porch swing.

Marek sat beside me. "What is it?"

I knotted my hands in my lap. It wasn't exactly a deep, dark secret, but I hadn't really talked about it before. It was the reason Mom wouldn't let me drive anymore.

"I was in a bad car accident last spring," I said. "The doctors couldn't believe how fast I healed."

Marek gazed at me with a look of concern. "What happened?"

I was surprised at how easy it was to open up to him. "We didn't have anything worth cooking in the house, so Mom sent me to the grocery store to pick up a few things. On the way home, a group of people from my high school ran a red light and hit me. I fractured my leg and broke a couple of ribs."

Marek gasped. "Ryn, I'm so sorry."

"I'm okay now," I assured him. "The funny thing about it is that the accident is one of the reasons I came here."

He tilted his head. "What do you mean?"

"I told you Mom always chooses where we move next."

Marek nodded.

"Well, when I was in the hospital, Mom asked if there was anything she could do to make things better. My only request was that I got to choose where we moved next. She agreed."

Not that she cared about any of that anymore. It was like she didn't even remember the accident happened.

"Instinct told me to take another route, but I ignored it," I said. "After that, I swore I would listen to my instincts more often. I guess my instinct led me here."

"*Grace* led you here," Marek emphasized.

His words struck me, and we both fell silent as we rocked back and forth on the porch swing. My mind flew through everything I'd learned over the past few days.

A thought suddenly occurred to me. If we had the power to heal, what had given Marek those scars on his back?

"How good is this healing power?" I asked.

"Pretty good." He shrugged. "I mean, it still hurt when you broke your leg, didn't it? You'd heal about three times faster, though."

"What about you? Do you heal the same as other Davina?" I thought about how Marek said some Davina didn't have full powers and wondered if he was one of them.

His features hardened. "It's not the perfect power. It doesn't heal everything. When things are bad enough..." He didn't finish.

My hand inched closer to his. "You can tell me."

He immediately swatted me away. "I told you before I didn't want to talk about it."

I stared at him in confusion. "Why did you show me if you didn't expect me to ask about it?"

"I didn't mean to." He grew irritated with each passing second.

"You told me everything else."

Marek stood abruptly. "Don't make me out to be the jerk, Ryn. Some of it you don't need to know. Maybe some of it I can't talk about."

I gaped at him. How could he go so quickly from being playful, fun-loving Marek to the irritated, closed-off guy standing in front of me?

"Go inside, Ryn," Marek said. It wasn't a suggestion. "Stay safe."

My heart sank. I hadn't meant to offend him. I was only trying to offer him comfort while trying to make sense of everything I'd learned so far.

I pressed my lips together and stood. I wasn't interested in picking a fight with him, so I did as he ordered.

But inside didn't offer me sanctuary.

I'd stepped away from one fight just to walk into another.

"Where have you been all afternoon?" Mom stood in the hall with her hands on her hips.

"I told you, I was hanging out with friends."

Mom pressed her lips into a thin line. "When you said friends, I thought you meant Allie. Who's the guy on the bike?"

Crap. She'd seen that.

"A friend," I insisted vaguely.

Is that what we were? Friends?

"He's a friend of Allie's," I clarified. "He offered to drive me home."

"Home from where?" she demanded.

"His house," I told her truthfully.

She crossed her arms over her chest. "That's completely irresponsible. I haven't met his parents."

"So?" I snapped. "I'm almost eighteen."

Mom's eyebrows raised so far they nearly touched her hairline. It was like she couldn't believe I had the audacity to point it out.

"You're not eighteen *yet*." She said it like it was a threat. "And until you are, I want to know where you're at."

Yeah, I doubted that was going to end once I turned eighteen.

"I don't want to have to worry about you," she said.

I wasn't buying that line. The truth was she wanted to control me as long as possible.

"I'm fine." I heard the lie in my own voice. Maybe she had a reason to worry, but it wasn't like I could tell her about what happened earlier.

By the way, Mom. I'm a Davina. Ever heard of them? I wasn't sure that was a conversation I wanted to have.

Best not, I told myself. *Mom's better off not knowing. She said goodbye to my insanity a long time ago. I don't need to drag her back into it.*

"And I don't want you riding a motorcycle," she demanded. "With a guy I don't even know, no less."

"There's nothing wrong with him. And he's a good

driver." No point in mentioning how fast he liked to drive. She'd never let me see him again.

"That doesn't matter," she argued. "Motorcycles are dangerous."

She was just jealous she didn't have a hot biker dude to run away with. She hadn't dated my whole life.

"How am I supposed to get around town, then?" I asked. "You won't let me drive."

She didn't seem to care that the accident wasn't my fault. I still couldn't get behind the wheel.

"You have two feet," she pointed out. "And there's a bicycle in the garden shed."

So my only options were to walk or bike anywhere I wanted to go? I was seventeen, not twelve.

I rolled my eyes. After everything that happened to me today, I didn't deserve this. "Whatever, I'm going to bed."

I stared up the stairs, but Mom apparently wasn't done chewing me out.

"Don't you use that tone with me," she scolded.

She huffed when I ignored her. She mumbled something about *teenagers*, but I didn't hear her as I hurried down the hall and into my room.

As soon as I fell down onto my bed, exhaustion consumed me. As I was falling asleep, something Fletcher had said resurfaced in my mind. He said he'd stop by on Monday to talk about my enrollment at Galen High.

I had a feeling after the way I just spoke to my mother, she wasn't going to be easy to convince.

letcher's visit couldn't come soon enough the next day. I waited eagerly in the living room that morning untangling balls of yarn Mom had bought from a garage sale. I didn't put up a fight when she'd asked me to do it because I wanted to stay on her good side.

By the time lunch hit, the doorbell still hadn't rung. I was starting to wonder if Fletcher would actually show.

Finally, the sound of footsteps on the porch caught my attention. I hopped up from the couch when the doorbell rang. The floorboards in Mom's home office creaked above my head.

I swung the door open a bit too quickly.

Fletcher greeted me with a smile.

I was surprised to see a woman standing beside him. She was a head shorter than him, with short dark hair and an air of professionalism in the way she held herself.

Fletcher wore his usual button-down collared shirt, and

the woman had on a navy pantsuit. They both looked strangely formal standing on my front porch.

"Miss Tyler," Fletcher greeted. "This is Mrs. Presley. We've come to discuss your enrollment."

"Yes, come in." I opened the door wider. "Just so you know, Mom doesn't know about the Davina." And I didn't intend to tell her.

Fletcher nodded in understanding.

The soft pad of footsteps on the stairs caught my attention. Mom descended the stairs slowly, and a confused expression settled on her face. I hadn't known how to tell her about Fletcher earlier. I thought he might have a better idea how to introduce the topic.

"Ah," Fletcher said, looking up at her. "You must be Mrs. Tyler. I'm Mr. Fletcher, an advisor at Galen High School. This is Mrs. Presley, our principal."

Mom reached the bottom of the stairs and stretched out a hand. "Hello. For what do I owe the pleasure?" She didn't sound anything like herself.

Mrs. Presley spoke for the first time. Her voice was at least a pitch higher than I expected. "We're partnered with Eagle Valley High to review incoming students' transcripts, and we believe that Kathryn would be a great fit at our school. We'd love to discuss the opportunity with you."

"Sure," my mother agreed, confusion still layered in her tone. "Why don't we have a seat in the living room? Can I get you anything?"

"No." Mrs. Presley sat on the couch and adjusted the coat on her pantsuit. "I'm fine, thank you."

"No, thank you," Fletcher told her.

Mom and I sat on the loveseat across from them.

Mrs. Presley opened a folder on her lap and glanced up at my mom with a smile. "I apologize that this is on short notice, but seeing as you just moved to the area, it's to be expected. As I said, we've reviewed Kathryn's transcript and think she would make a great fit at Galen High."

She glanced back down at her papers. "Her grades are good, all A's and B's, and she's been involved in extracurriculars all throughout high school."

I didn't know what record she was looking at, but it couldn't have been that accurate, unless she counted the prom committee at my last school.

"I'm sorry," my mom stopped her. "Public school has served Kathryn well her whole life. What is it that Galen thinks they can offer her?"

My jaw nearly dropped to the floor at her words. Did she not want me to go? I had to go. I needed all the help I could get if I wanted to learn what I was capable of.

"But Mom," I started.

Fletcher was already speaking. "We have a very intense curriculum that would suit a student of Kathryn's talent."

"I apologize," Mom said. "I know my daughter is talented, but—"

"Mom," I interjected. "I want to go."

She stared at me. "Is it because Allie goes there? You'll make new friends at Eagle Valley High just as well."

"It's a smaller school," I tried. It sounded unconvincing, even to me. "I'll have an easier time getting to know people and connecting with my teachers. I've always liked smaller schools anyway."

Mom pressed her lips together. "Maybe we should discuss this a little more."

Mrs. Presley shifted uncomfortably in her seat. "I'm sorry, but is there something wrong with our school?"

Mom looked shocked. "No, I just—we just…" She glanced at me like I might be able to help her find the right words. Her confession came out in a near whisper. "We don't have money for a private school."

The two Davina across from me relaxed.

"Not to worry," Mrs. Presley assured her. "Kathryn is eligible for a full scholarship. It won't cost you a penny more than putting her in public school."

I hadn't thought of the costs, but it's not like there was any other option. I was a Davina. I belonged at Galen High.

The thought sent a nervous shiver down my spine—in a surprisingly good way. Mom and I moved around so much that I never felt like I belonged anywhere. For the first time in my life, I did.

I wasn't alone. The demons weren't just in my head. Sure, I'd been able to ignore them for the better part of a decade, but they were always there, lurking in my peripheral vision, their voices filling an otherwise quiet room. The other Davina knew what that was like.

More than that, the demons didn't come into Eagle Valley. I could stay here and forget about them.

"Can I go, Mom?" I pleaded.

She didn't answer for a moment. "We should really talk about this more, in private."

"But there's only two weeks left before school starts!" I argued.

I knew my mom. She was going to put off talking about it for so long that I'd miss enrolling by the first day of school. She never let me have anything I wanted.

"If you need the time to think about it, we can leave the paperwork here," Mrs. Presley offered. "You can take your time reading through it. I'll write my cell number down so you can call with any questions."

I gave her a reluctant smile. I felt anything but cheerful. "Thanks."

"Yes, thank you," Mom said. "We'll consider it."

Sure we will, I thought sarcastically.

Mrs. Presley stood and shook both of our hands. She held onto mine a little longer. "We hope to see you soon."

I smiled back. "Thank you."

Fletcher shook my mom's hand and then mine. What felt like far too soon, they left.

Mom turned to me after leading them out the door. She crossed her arms over her chest and looked at me with a hard expression.

Here we go again.

I bit my lower lip. "So, can I go to Galen?"

I expected Mom to sit on the couch across from me so we could talk about it, but she remained standing.

"Why are you so interested in going?" she asked with an edge to her tone.

Because I'm a Davina like the rest of them.

"Have you seen Galen High?" I asked rhetorically. "It's beautiful. It'd be cool to go there my senior year."

She pressed her lips into such a thin line that they practically disappeared. "Does that boy go there?"

"What boy?" I asked innocently.

"The one with the motorcycle."

Oh. *That* boy.

"Yeah, but that's not why—"

Her brows shot up. "Oh, *that's not why*. I was a teenager once, too, you know."

Oh, hells no. She wasn't keeping me from Galen High just to keep me away from a boy.

I shot up out of my seat. "You don't want me to go because you think I'm *whoring around?*"

Her nostrils flared. So much for staying on her good side.

"I never said that!" she defended.

My eyebrow twitched challengingly. "You didn't have to."

Mom dropped her arms to her sides and huffed. "Kathryn, you're being ridiculous."

I rolled my eyes. "So I guess that's a no. I'm not going to Galen High."

"I'm still considering it, but if you keep up this attitude, the answer *will* be no."

"There's no reason not to let me go," I insisted. "They're giving me a scholarship."

"And I said we'd think about it."

I huffed. "You never let me do anything I want to do."

"Oh, really? Who chose to move us to Eagle Valley?"

"*You* chose to move us," I emphasized. "You *always* choose to move us. We move so often I never get a chance to make any real friends. Allie's the best friend I've had in over a decade, and now you're taking my last chance at making real friends away."

I stormed past her into the hall. Eager for a door to slam, I turned to the first one and slammed it behind me as hard as I could.

17

I pounded down the steps into the basement. Next to the washer stood two full laundry baskets. Mom definitely wasn't going to let me go to Galen if she saw my laundry still wasn't finished.

Gritting my teeth, I dumped the entire contents of the first basket in the washer, not caring about mixing the whites with the colors. I tossed in some soap without measuring it and slammed the lid shut.

My skin grew hot in anger. I barely knew what I was doing when I swung my foot angrily at the shelf in the corner. A gallon of paint teetered on the edge. I just barely caught it before it smashed into the concrete floor. My foot throbbed, and my heart raced.

I sank to the dusty floor and set the paint can beside me. I wanted nothing more than to cry—to scream—but even as I buried my face in my hands, nothing came.

I curled myself into a ball on the floor.

Why was Mom so selfish? She always got to do what *she*

wanted to do but never seemed to care about my feelings. Forget the fact that I was destined to save the world and Galen High could actually help me do it. She had too much pride to allow me the chance.

Maybe I'd sneak off and go there anyway.

A banging in the corner of the room pulled my attention from my self-pity. I glanced up to find the washer violently shaking, indicating an uneven load. I reluctantly rose from the floor and walked over to it. I threw open the lid and rearranged the clothes inside.

Turning back to the shelf behind me, I sighed heavily. It didn't matter how long I sat there in the cold, damp basement. Sooner or later, I had to face her again.

I picked up the can of paint I'd knocked over and went to place it back on the shelf, but something caught my eye. I lowered myself to peek past the shelf to the wall behind it. I had to tilt my head to each side several times to make out what I'd found.

What looked like a carving of an eagle had been etched into the stone of the house's old foundation.

Another thing to add to the list of traits that give this house character, I thought.

Only after a moment of staring at it did I realize something was off. The figure had the wings of an eagle but the body of a woman. For a moment, I could almost imagine it was me.

The thought settled in my mind.

Forget Mom. Forget Galen High. I was a freaking Davina. I could fly. I didn't have to take this crap.

I shoved the paint can back in its place and pounded up

the steps, not stopping until I made it to my bedroom. I stripped off my shirt and tossed it in the corner then flung my dresser drawer open to find a sports bra and a racerback tank.

I can do this, I told myself. My breaths grew shallow, and my hands shook as I tensed my muscles.

Come on, Ryn.

I squeezed my eyes closed and concentrated on my back as if wings would sprout from it simply by wishing for it. After about a minute, I opened them, more frustrated than before.

I gripped onto the back of the chair in front of my desk so hard that my knuckles turned white. I didn't quite like what I saw in the mirror. Despite my quickened heart rate, my face looked drained of color, and my eyes drooped.

"What are you doing, Ryn?" I asked my reflection. *I'm not cut out for this.*

The longer I stared at my reflection, the more I got the feeling that something was missing. I could picture myself with the wings Marek had shown me earlier. A strong desire to fly—like I'd felt when Allie and I rolled down the hill—overcame me.

My mom could move me all across the states. She could refuse to send me to Galen High. But she couldn't control *this.*

This one was all me.

Something in the mirror caught my eye. The studs in my ears were all wrong for this.

I quickly slipped them out of my ears and threw open my drawer to find my pair of angel wing studs. A sense of comfort washed over me when I put them on. They reminded me of the carving in the basement.

I've got this.

I closed my eyes again and took a deep breath. My mind focused on the angel wing earrings like I actually thought they might hold some power that could bring me the strength to overcome this.

I flexed my shoulders again. This time, my hands didn't quiver. Tension built within my muscles, and a tingling sensation radiated across my back.

Slowly, I opened my eyes. What I saw in the mirror took my breath away.

Two glorious white wings rose behind me. Each one was as tall as I was. Fluffy white feathers lined the top of the wings and grew steadily larger until they reached the size of my hand at the bottom.

I twisted to get a better look and noticed immediately how the white feathers seemed to shimmer purple in the light. I couldn't take my eyes off them.

A knock came at my bedroom door.

Shit.

18

I whirled around so fast that my right wing caught the chair and knocked it to the floor.

"Don't come in, Mom!"

How do I make these things disappear?

"It's me," a different voice called back. "Allie."

I relaxed.

"Your mom let me in," she said. "Are you okay?"

"Yeah. You can come in."

Allie pushed the door open. Her eyes instantly grew to twice their size. "Oh my gosh! You did it!"

I couldn't help but beam.

"This is great!" she exclaimed. "You're making progress."

I shot back a shy smile. "Thanks, but how do I... you know... make them go away?"

The corners of Allie's lips twitched like she was trying not to laugh.

"Not that I want to," I said quickly. "I just thought you were my mom, and I realized I didn't know how to."

"You just relax," she said simply.

"Great," I mumbled, stealing another glance in the mirror. "These things will never go away."

Allie laughed. She took a deep inhale and spoke softly on the exhale. "Just… relax."

I mimicked her patterned breathing. Slowly, the wings began to shrink behind my back. I turned my back to the mirror to inspect my skin. Wrapping my arm around my body, I felt the area where the wings had grown out of. It was completely smooth.

I turned back to Allie. "I don't get it."

She sat on the bed and tossed her dark hair over her shoulder. "What don't you get?"

"It didn't hurt or anything." I took a seat beside her on my white comforter.

She furrowed her brow. "No. Why would it?"

"Well, I—" I paused. "I saw Marek's scars."

"Oh, yeah," Allie said like it was no big deal. "Those are totally different."

"How'd he get them?" I burned to know.

She bit her lip. "Sorry, but it's not my place to tell. I don't really know the full story."

I got the sense that no matter how much I begged her for information, Allie wasn't going to spill.

Allie eyed me curiously after a brief silence. "Are you okay?"

I thought about it for a moment. "Yeah. Mom and I just had a huge fight. She doesn't want me to go to Galen."

Allie let out a breath in disbelief. I half expected her to call my mom out for being a bitch.

"Did you tell her about the demon?" Allie asked.

"No. I haven't told her any of it. She would never believe me."

"Why not?"

I sighed and resituated myself on the bed. "When I was little, I told my mom I could see the demons. I didn't call them that, though. I didn't know what they were then."

Allie nodded along in understanding.

"She told me I was imagining things," I continued. "She sent me to three different therapists before I lied and told her I'd stopped seeing them."

Some of the tension I constantly held in my body eased. It felt good to open up to her.

Allie's eyes widened. "I'm so sorry, Ryn. Your mom might be more willing to let you go to Galen if she knew the truth. I could help back you up."

I shook my head. Allie's gesture was nice, but I wasn't ready to talk to my mom about any of this.

"If she knew a demon attacked you and that you were in danger—" Allie started, but I cut her off.

"I don't want to talk about that." My voice came off harsher than I intended.

Allie looked at me in confusion, and then realization dawned. "Ryn, what did he do to you?"

"He attacked me," I said simply. "Like Marek told you."

"Marek was pretty vague about it," Allie said.

I twisted my hands in my lap. "It could've been worse."

"That doesn't mean you're not allowed to feel something," Allie said gently. "Someone will always have it worse than you. That doesn't invalidate your feelings."

I sat silent, letting her words sink in. If I was going to tell anyone, Allie would be my first choice.

"His hands were all over me," I admitted. "If Marek hadn't come to my rescue…"

Allie drew in an audible breath and leaned over to pull me in to an embrace.

I inhaled the comforting scent of her cherry blossom perfume. It was like hugging the sister I never had.

"The demons are evil," Allie said as she pulled away. "They killed my mom."

My heart broke. I knew her mom wasn't around, but I never knew why.

"Kyle's dad, too," Allie said. "I guess that's why we work well together. We both lost something to the demons."

"Allie, I'm so sorry." I pulled her back into a hug.

"Don't worry about it," she said. "It happened a long time ago."

"Is that why you want to be a Protector?" I asked.

Allie nodded shyly. "The demons hurt enough people as it is."

Her words hung uncomfortably in the air.

Finally, I broke the silence. "What'd you come over for?"

A smile twitched at the corner of her lips. "Well, it looks like you already figured out your wings. Do you want to try flying?"

My heart flipped at the thought of flying for the first time.

"Yes!" I answered eagerly.

If Mom lets me out of the house.

Allie rose from the bed. "Let's go. We'll meet the guys at the valley."

I paused momentarily. "The valley?"

"Yeah, that's where we fly."

Which meant I had to walk through those woods again.

"Isn't there another place in town we can go?" I asked.

Allie shook her head. "Not anywhere we won't be spotted."

I bit my lower lip.

"Hey," Allie said gently. "You're going to be all right. We'll be there with you."

Her words were incredibly reassuring.

I gave her a timid smile. "Thanks, Allie."

She stood from the bed. "Ready for your first flight lesson?"

19

Given everything that happened recently, I should've been screaming while someone dragged me away to a mental institution. Instead, I was excited about my first flying lesson. Flying was sure to make everything better.

By some miracle, Mom agreed to let me go—and even said I could stay the night at Allie's house. Something I'd said to her earlier must've stuck.

Allie and I took her car and parked across from Galen High.

My fingers quivered against the door handle. I stared past the edge of the school to the trailhead that led to the valley. My mouth went dry when I thought about what had happened the last time I was here.

A knock came at my window, startling me.

"You ready?" Marek asked. I hadn't noticed his arrival.

I forced my heart rate to slow and opened the door. "Yeah."

Allie glanced at her phone. "Kyle's already waiting for us."

"You okay?" Marek asked when we began walking.

"Yeah, I'm fine," I told him, but I could feel my face had drained of color.

"Don't worry," Marek said in a low whisper so Allie couldn't hear. "I'm not going to let you out of my sight this time, okay?"

As if to prove I could trust him, Marek grabbed my hand and squeezed it. I stared into his blue eyes.

Marek lifted one side of his mouth into a twisted smile. "Let's go have some fun."

"Are you two coming?" Allie called from several paces away.

I snapped my attention back to her. Marek dropped my hand, and it suddenly felt cold. I didn't realize I'd slowed at the entrance to the trail until Marek placed a hand on my back.

"It's okay," he whispered in my ear.

I needed to believe him, so I pushed forward.

I couldn't stand the silence. "Hey, Marek?"

"Yeah?"

"I'm curious. What all can Davina do? We have wings, and this sort of... magic."

"Well," Marek said, "it's not as cool as it sounds, I'll tell you that. Mostly, it's a weapon. We can stun demons with it, just like they can do the same to us."

"How else are they similar to us?" I asked curiously. My eyes remained on the path.

Marek shrugged. "They have wings."

My brows shot up. I shouldn't have been surprised, but I'd never seen them. "Really?"

"Well, yeah. Theirs are black, ours are white." He shrugged like it wasn't a big deal.

"What about the cloaks?" I asked. "Why do they wear them?"

"It's about tradition," he explained. "Originally, it was to set themselves apart. We used to wear white robes for the same reason. We eventually dropped the robe practice, but at least we had other clothes to wear. The demon's cloaks come from material brought from their realm long ago, when the portals were still open. They don't have any other choice."

"Kyle!" Allie shouted in excitement ahead of us.

I didn't have a chance to ask more questions as Marek and I broke through the trees into the clearing.

I noticed movement at the far end of the valley. What looked like the largest bird I'd ever seen soared near the tree line. It was unlike any other bird in the sky, though, with the body of a man and the wings of an eagle.

Kyle spread his wings wide and glided toward us gracefully. Air rushed by his wings when he landed, and the grass rustled beneath us. Kyle brushed his dark hair out of his eyes. His wings were bigger than Marek's, but he wasn't quite as toned.

"Anyone want to race?" Kyle asked.

"You're on!" Allie quickly stripped off her cardigan.

I watched in awe as white feathers sprouted from her back and grew into beautiful wings. Though my wings shimmered a slight purple, Allie's had a bluish tint to them. It matched the subtle blue shine in her black hair.

She lit up with a smile. She truly looked like an angel.

Without another word, Allie and Kyle raced to the edge of the hill and took off in unison. Their wings nearly touched as they spread out beyond their arm span.

I kept my eyes on Allie in wonder. She pumped her wings and shot forward above the landscape. She flew so effortlessly that it was as if magic kept her afloat. Even with the sun hidden behind an overcast sky, I could still make out the blue shimmer in her wings from a distance.

My heart felt as if it was soaring alongside her. The more I watched, the more excitement filled my chest.

Allie's wings were smaller than Kyle's, but that seemed to work to her advantage. She was much quicker than him. She was also several inches shorter and fifty pounds lighter, so she didn't have to work as hard to keep herself airborne.

As soon as they reached the other end of the valley, they both turned around and headed back toward Marek and me. Allie sped up until her ankle was in line with Kyle's head.

"Should we move?" I glanced at Marek to find him smiling at the couple.

"No, they'll be fine."

"Are you sure? They're coming right for us."

Marek laughed. "They know what they're doing."

I contemplated diving out of the way as Allie made her landing, but Marek placed an arm around me, forcing me to stay. My first instinct was to be annoyed with him, but then his arm relaxed against my shoulder. I relaxed, too.

Allie hit the ground and immediately tumbled into a summer-sault to slow her momentum. She landed on her feet and shot her fists into the air in victory. Her wings had vanished.

"You suck!" she gloated when Kyle landed.

He laughed. "You know I let you win."

Allie rolled her eyes. "Whatever."

"You ready for a go?" Kyle asked. It took me a second to realize he was talking to me.

My eyebrows rose. "Me? I'm not racing."

Kyle smiled. "Why not? I need to beat a girl one of these days."

Marek jumped to my defense. "Give her a break, Kyle. She's never flown before."

"That's why I'll finally be able to beat someone." He stood so confidently that I wasn't convinced he was as bad as he was suggesting.

"Relax," Allie told him. "You beat Casey all the time."

"Yeah, well, Casey's not as good as she thinks she is," Kyle said.

Even I could've guessed that based on my first impres-sion of her, and I hadn't even seen her fly yet.

"I'm not going to race, but I'd like to try flying." I spoke to no one in particular. "How do we do this?"

A smile twitched at the corner of Marek's lips. "You know how birds learn to fly by being pushed out of the nest?"

"Yeah…"

Marek raised his brows.

"What? You're not going to push me off a cliff, are you?"

Everyone laughed beside me.

"No," Marek assured me. "But it really doesn't get much simpler than that. Allie says you've figured out your wings?"

I nodded.

"Well, let's see them," Kyle insisted.

I bit my lip and glanced between my friends. I didn't want to make a fool out of myself.

"We'll all do it together," Allie suggested. She flexed her shoulders, and her wings returned.

"Okay," I agreed.

Beside me, Marek stripped down to expose his toned torso.

Note to self: Keep your eyes off Hot Stuff while airborne—unless you plan to crash and burn. He's too damn distracting.

"Ready?" Marek asked.

I noticed his fingers twitch in my direction like he was about to take my hand. At the last second, he pulled away.

I nodded and then took a deep breath, flexing my back. I felt the afternoon air brush across my feathers. This time, it was easier to let them out now that I knew what it felt like. I stretched them as wide as I could.

I'd never felt more refreshed than I did in that moment… like something had been missing my whole life, and for the first time, I'd embraced it.

I turned my attention back to my friends. Allie stared, Kyle rose his eyebrows, and Marek smiled.

"What?" I pulled my wings closer to me.

Allie blinked several times. "There's just something… magical about seeing you discover your wings. You look so happy."

I realized I was smiling. "I never knew what I was missing."

"Ready to give it a try?" Kyle asked.

I nodded.

"Start by trying to flap your wings," Marek suggested. "Don't try to take off. Just move them to get a feel for it."

I did as I was instructed. It felt like I'd grown another set of arms, but strangely, the movement came naturally.

"How does it feel?" Allie asked enthusiastically.

I glanced behind my shoulder to watch my wings move up and down. If it wasn't for the tightening and relaxing of my muscles with every motion, I'd never believe they were my own.

"It feels great," I told her.

"You ready to try flying?" Marek asked.

I took a deep breath. "I'm ready."

"We'll fly alongside you," Marek explained. "One on either side and one in the back. That way, if you feel you might fall, we can catch you."

I nodded.

"It helps to get a running start," he continued. "Once you do, take a big leap and spread your wings out to glide. Flap to gain height, and tilt your body to change direction. It's not too hard to get once you're in the air. The trouble is finding the courage to get off the ground." He smiled at his last comment. "Remember, this is the easy part of being a Davina."

"Ugh. Don't remind me," I complained. "That means I have a lot more to learn."

Marek laughed. "Yeah, but you'll catch on quickly. Let's do this together."

Marek stood to my right while Allie situated herself on my left. Kyle took the spot behind me.

"Run, jump, and spread your wings," Marek reminded me. "Don't forget to flap them once you start losing height."

I rolled my eyes. "I'm not a child. I've got this."

Though my voice came out strong and commanding, I wasn't sure. Frankly, I was afraid I might break a leg, but I couldn't sit back without at least giving it a shot.

"Okay," Marek agreed. "On the count of three?"

I took off toward the hill before he finished the countdown. I saw Marek and Allie racing alongside me in my peripheral vision. Just as the hill dropped to a sharp decline, I dug my feet into the dirt and launched my body forward, spreading my wings out at the peak of my jump.

The ground dropped away from me. And so did my stomach.

My tummy tickled in the same way it felt to drive too fast over a hill. It was like someone flipped off the switch to gravity and my insides remained suspended high within my abdomen.

"Flap your wings!" Marek reminded me.

I immediately followed his instruction after realizing how quickly I was losing height. Wind rushed through my hair, tangling it into a wild mess. But I didn't care. I welcomed the air beneath my wings as it pressed against me and kept me afloat.

I dared to steal a glance below me. The base of the valley seemed miles away.

My heart slammed against my rib cage in exhilaration, and a satisfying tingle spread across my skin. It was the kind of rush that came with riding a rollercoaster. Only better.

I flapped my wings harder, daring to press the limits.

"Don't go above the tree line!" Allie warned. She had to shout for me to hear her.

I did as I was told. Instead of focusing on gaining height, I turned my attention to pressing forward.

I didn't fly as gracefully as the rest of them. Each flap of my wings seemed to shoot me into the air. The next moment, I'd fall several feet before counteracting gravity with another flap of my wings. At the very least, I managed to stay airborne, and my fear of breaking a bone slowly eased.

Once we reached the opposite end of the valley, Marek called to me. "We're going to circle around and try landing. Follow my lead. We'll glide and land at the bottom of the valley."

"Okay," I called back.

Marek leaned his body to the left.

I followed him. Where he made turning look effortless, I had to flap my wings double time to maintain my height.

As soon as he was headed in the right direction, he spread his wings wide and began to glide through the air.

I copied him and found myself descending toward the ground slowly. I actually felt for a moment like I might look graceful while doing it.

"Bend your knees when you land," Marek shouted my way. "It'll help absorb the impact."

As the ground grew closer, I feared we may be coming in too fast.

Allie charged ahead to demonstrate the landing. At the last second, she pulled her body back and swooped her wings up, landing perfectly on two feet.

I braced myself for impact. Though I did my best to mimic her motions, I stumbled and fell face-first into the grass. The inside of my right arm skidded along the ground. I pulled my wings back in and flipped over to examine my arm. Dirt had embedded itself into my raw skin.

"You okay?" Marek asked, landing beside me.

"Yeah, I'm fine." I bit back a cry as I tried to dust off the dirt. It stung.

"It was a good first flight," he said. "A few months at it and you could be the best flyer at Galen High."

I rolled my eyes, knowing he was just saying that to encourage me. "Don't use up all your compliments at once."

Marek smirked. "I'm sure I can come up with a few more."

Allie knelt beside me to take a look at my arm. "Doesn't look too bad. By tomorrow, there won't be any evidence of your landing."

"Ha ha," I said dryly.

"Uh," Kyle said to get our attention. "I wouldn't be so sure of that. We have witnesses."

We followed his gaze to find Blonde Bitch and her two body guards staring down at us from the top of the hill.

20

Casey wasted no time making her way down to us. Her wings spread out behind her as she glided our way. She landed gracefully at my feet. She plastered a fake smile on her face and clapped her hands in a condescending manner.

Troy and Trenton landed behind her.

"Impressive." Casey dragged out the word, clearly not meaning it. She turned her attention to Allie. "So this is the talent you were talking about. You guys *really* have a shot at beating us this year."

Marek helped me to my feet.

"Bite me, Barbie." The words came out before I could think to stop them.

Casey blinked rapidly. "Excuse me?"

I glanced at Allie. Her eyebrows were raised in surprise.

I dusted the dirt off my jeans while I spoke. "I'm sure you weren't that great the first time you flew, either."

She narrowed her eyes at me. "I was, like, five."

"And?" I challenged, finally standing upright.

Casey opened her mouth once then closed it without saying anything. She rolled her eyes so heavily I thought they might fall out of her skull. "Whatever. Clearly they've already turned you against me." She shot both Allie and Kyle a disgusted look.

I crossed my arms. "Believe it or not, we don't sit around talking about you. We have more important things to do."

"Right. I heard there was a demon hanging around town. Word is he wants you. What'd you do to upset a demon?" Casey looked positively pleased with herself.

How did she know?

"That's none of your business," Allie snarled. She took a step forward, but Kyle placed a hand on her shoulder to hold her back.

Casey eyed her with loathing. "It's *my* dad out there hunting this thing. To protect *you*."

"To protect *everyone*," Allie pointed out.

"He's not the only one out there," Kyle said.

I realized Casey's dad must've been one of the Davina Fletcher had said he'd recruited to help.

"I still don't think he should be risking himself," Casey said.

Marek stepped forward. "Everyone relax."

I crossed my arms over my chest. "If your dad's out there, why hasn't he found him yet?"

Casey pursed her lips but didn't answer.

"Calm down, Casey," Marek insisted. "We're all Davina. We're on the same side."

Casey raised her blond eyebrows like she couldn't believe he'd suggest such a thing. "Competition is a good thing. It makes us stronger."

"But it doesn't make us enemies," Marek stated.

A muscle in Casey's jaw popped. "No, James, it doesn't. That one's on you."

An uncomfortable silence filled the air.

I glanced to Allie like she might have an answer.

"This is a waste of time," Casey finally said. "Enjoy your training session, but don't expect to have the place to yourself forever. We'll be back later. Come on, guys. Let's go."

She pushed past Troy and Trenton, knocking one of them in the shoulder—I couldn't remember which was which. Then she spread her wings to fly back to the top of the valley. The group disappeared through the trees.

It seemed to take a lifetime as we watched them go. The uncomfortable silence still hung in the air where we stood. I wasn't about to be the first to speak.

"What a bitch," Allie muttered under her breath.

"Don't call her that," Marek countered.

Kyle scoffed. "Why not? It's true."

Marek shook his head and ran his fingers through his brown hair. "It's rude."

"You don't have to be so bossy all the time," Allie said, raising her voice. "You don't still have feelings for her, do you?"

My jaw dropped.

"Of course not! I never had feelings for her," Marek argued.

"Sure you didn't," Allie said like she didn't believe him.

I looked to Kyle, hoping he might be able to explain. He shook his head, suggesting I shouldn't even ask.

"It's true." Irritation entered Marek's tone. "Can we just forget about it?"

Marek turned to me. "Ryn, I think we should move on to something else. You did really well with the flying, but it's not going to help you much in combat. Remember that demons can fly, too. We've got to get you comfortable using your magic, and you should know some hand-to-hand stuff in case you need it."

I started to agree with him, but Allie grabbed my arm and cut me off.

"Excuse us a moment." She dragged me several paces away.

"What?" I hissed.

"Would you rather Kyle and I leave?" she whispered.

I looked at her in confusion. "Why would I want that?"

"If Marek's really forgotten about Casey, you have a chance with him. It'll give you two a chance to get to know each other better." Allie wiggled her eyebrows. She was playing matchmaker again.

A blush rose to my cheeks. "You think I have a chance with him?"

Allie scoffed. "Girl, I've never seen him look at someone the way he looks at you."

I glanced over at Marek. He spoke to Kyle but kept his gaze on me. My heart flipped inside my chest like I was flying again.

I let my hair hide my face from him as I turned back to Allie. "He looks at me in a special way?"

Allie nodded like she couldn't believe I hadn't noticed. "If you want to spend some time alone with him, we'll give you space."

"I—uh—" I didn't know what to say. Of course I wanted to get to know him more, but was now the right time?

"You can do whatever you want," I told her.

She smiled wide. "Great. I'll see you later tonight. We can paint our nails and read through gossip magazines while you dish the juicy details."

I wasn't actually sure if she was kidding or not.

Allie turned back to Marek and Kyle. "Kyle, we have to go."

He looked at her in confusion. "Why?"

"I just realized…" She didn't finish her lie. She simply took his hand and led him away toward the stairs.

As soon as they were out of earshot, I turned back to Marek. "So, about Casey… I feel like I'm totally missing something."

He sighed heavily and shoved his hands in his pockets. "It's kind of a long story."

"I have time."

He gazed down at his feet, avoiding my gaze. "Okay… When I was new at Galen, Casey and I trained together. Long story short, I thought we were friends. She thought we were more."

The idea of Marek and Casey together made me want to puke.

Marek raked his fingers through his hair. "After I turned her down, she became pretty difficult to work with.

She's been trying to prove how much better she is since then."

"So, you two weren't a thing?" Hope entered my tone.

Marek shrugged. "I guess I can see where I might've led her on, but I didn't mean anything by it."

"Does she still like you?"

Say no.

"God, no. I don't think she even realizes why she hates me so much. She's not good at letting things go, but half the time, she doesn't know what she's holding onto. I just —" Marek shifted his weight between his feet.

"What is it?"

He didn't look at me. "I don't have an easy time opening up to people. I think Casey took that personally."

I stared into his face sympathetically and spoke softly. "I'm sorry."

Marek continued to avoid my gaze. "For what? You didn't do anything."

"I did. I was a jerk to you."

I shouldn't have tried to push him into telling me about his scars. Involuntarily, I reached out to him, hoping it would get him to look at me.

He didn't pull away like I was afraid he might. Instead, he let me run my hand down his arm until our fingers entwined. He took a breath and gazed down at me. Our bodies inched closer together.

"Believe me," he said, "you're anything but a jerk. I was impossible to work with when I first came here."

I quieted, hoping he would elaborate. Instead, silence settled over the valley once again as he stared down into my eyes. His gaze flickered to my lips for a moment, and I swallowed hard. I was sure he could feel my fingers quivering in his.

This was it. He was going to kiss me.

Marek closed the distance between us in what felt like slow motion. Our eyes connected, and my breathing grew shallow. The sound of my own heartbeat echoed in my ears.

The kiss I'd been expecting never came. Marek let out a breath of shock, and then he crumbled to the ground, unconscious.

21

Instinct overcame me, and I dropped to my knees next to Marek. A moment later, I was on full alert, glancing around the valley frantically in search of an explanation.

The answer stood at the top of the hill with his feet spread apart in a confident stance. Another dark fireball was already forming in his fist.

Dorian.

Anger flared through my body, and my skin heated. What felt like an electric current ran down my right arm. The white essence I'd conjured last Friday night had returned. My anger subsided for only a moment, replaced instead by a wave of pride and victory.

The sound of flapping wings snapped my attention back to Dorian. I'd let myself be distracted for too long.

Two feathery midnight-black wings rose out from somewhere in the tangle of robes he wore. He landed just yards away from me.

I didn't know what to do next. With Marek on the ground, I felt so alone.

I knew exactly what Marek would tell me to do, though. *Kill him.*

I can't, I told myself.

The electricity in my palm fizzled away.

Shit. Dorian wouldn't care if I was unarmed and defenseless. He'd probably have more fun this way.

I gave one last glance down at my hand, but no matter how badly I wanted it, my essence didn't return.

"Why don't you lower your hood?" I challenged. I knew words were the only weapon I had at the moment. "Face me like a man."

Dorian took a step toward me, sending my heart racing.

"I'm not a man." He laughed. "You know that."

Keep him talking. Keep him talking. I didn't know what to say, but I had to come up with something. And fast.

"And you know what *I* am," I stated.

I could tell I piqued his interest by the way his hand twitched.

"So what if I do?" he asked.

"You saw what I did to your friend. Are you *really* sure you want your revenge like this? You know what I'm capable of."

I tried to sound confident, but I wasn't. Dorian sustained a fireball in his hand. It would take only a second for him to knock me out and strangle me to death.

He let out a bone-chilling laugh. "You think I'm doing this for revenge?"

I accidentally let my voice falter. "If not revenge, then what?"

"I know you have the power of an Original. No other angel I've seen has magic like yours." Dorian relaxed his hand, and the magic in it disappeared. "I'm not here to hurt you."

I forced down the lump in my throat so I could speak past it. His words didn't help reassure me. "Then why *are* you here?"

He held his head high. "I've come to convince you to join me."

Well, damn. That's definitely not what I expected to hear.

"Join you?" I asked curiously.

"With your magic, the Aedes could grow strong. We could build an army together, one that could win this war and stop the bloodshed."

I narrowed my eyes suspiciously. "How does my magic help you?"

"An Aedes child with your kind of power could lead an army. With enough of them, we'd be unstoppable. And with me as their father, I'd become a god to my people."

My breath froze in my chest. This was way worse than I could have ever imagined. Dorian wasn't planning to kill me. He was planning to turn me into a baby cannon.

Out of the corner of my eye, I noticed Marek's arm twitch beneath me. He was starting to wake. I had to keep Dorian talking.

I inched back a step. "What makes you think I'd go along with this?"

"Because one way or another, I *will* have you." He sounded so sure of himself. "You don't have a choice. You can either come with me nicely… or I'll make you."

I scoffed. "You think you'll be a hero to your people, yet you don't fight like it. Attacking me when no one else is around? Knocking my friend out to make sure he can't save me this time? You're not a hero. You're a *coward*."

Dorian laughed again. "We'll see about that." He stretched his hand out to conjure another fireball.

"You just made one mistake," I said with a raise of my eyebrow.

The orb in his hand instantly stopped growing.

"And what's that?" he growled.

Marek's voice came as I knew it would. "You kept talking."

Marek leapt to his feet and shot a white fireball at Dorian. A smile spread across my face before Marek's magic even made it to Dorian, but that smile quickly faded when Dorian dodged out of the way. Marek was quick and had already sent another ball of magic toward him.

Dorian ducked out of the way again. He launched himself forward and knocked Marek to the ground. His wings disappeared beneath his cloak. He pulled a fist back and smashed it into Marek's nose. Blood spirted across the grass.

Before I knew what I was doing, my foot connected with Dorian's ribs. Hard. He grunted and rolled off of Marek.

My nostrils flared, and my breath came in shallow heaves. "Do *not* touch him!"

Dorian pushed himself up, and his hood fell. Those dark, callous eyes glared at me like he was trying to burn a hole through my soul.

An electric tingle spread through my fingers. I was surprised to see a purple fireball form in my hand. I glanced to Marek uncertainly.

He held a hand over his bleeding nose. His eyes widened in urgency, but I hesitated.

If Marek had my powers, Dorian would be dead already. Despite how much Dorian terrified and angered me, I couldn't bring myself to do it.

"Go!" I shouted at Dorian.

I held a weapon in my hand that could end him in a heartbeat. What was he still doing hanging around?

Dorian smiled sardonically. "You don't have the guts to kill me."

"Do you really want to stick around and find out?" I threatened. "Get out of here before I change my mind!"

Dorian sighed in a way that sounded like he was mocking me. "I'd hoped you'd come willingly. It would've made this a lot easier." He rose to his feet. Dark feathery wings grew out of his back again. "Remember, Little Angel, I'm not giving you a choice."

He launched himself into the air. His wings flapped vigorously, carrying him away from us.

Marek wiped the blood from his face and rose to his feet.

"Don't say it," I warned before he had a chance to speak.

I could already tell by the hard expression on his face what he wanted to say.

I shouldn't have let Dorian go.

But I wasn't going to make myself—or Marek—into a killer.

Dorian had to realize his plan would never work. My magic was stronger than his. I could only hope that would keep him away.

Marek tore his gaze from the horizon as soon as Dorian disappeared. He took my hand.

"Come on," he said in a commanding tone. "Let's go."

We raced up the stairs and down the trail without saying a word. My legs burned in protest. I sucked in large gulps of air without really feeling like I was breathing. Marek slowed and pulled out his phone near the end of the trail.

"We need to meet up," he barked into the phone. "Now." He paused for a moment. "At the school." He punched the screen so hard I thought he might crack it.

"Who—" I inhaled a deep breath. "Who are we going to meet?"

Marek was already scrolling through his phone for another number. He ignored me and pulled the phone to his ear. "Hey, Allie. Something happened again. We're meeting up with Fletcher. You and Kyle should come, too." It didn't sound like a suggestion.

He hung up and slipped his phone back in his pocket.

"I'm sorry," he said through labored breaths.

"For what?"

"I promised you nothing would happen. I just didn't think that... He must've been watching us, waiting until we were... vulnerable." Marek's eyes fell on the school building in the distance. "Come on. We need to tell the others."

22

*A*llie and Kyle hadn't made it far. They were engaged in what looked like a heated conversation next to her vehicle. Allie stopped mid-sentence when she noticed our approach.

"What the hell?" She rushed to us. "We were *just* with you guys! What could've happened in the last five minutes?"

"Dorian." The name barely came out past the lump in my throat.

"Dorian?" she asked.

"The demon," Marek clarified with a scowl.

Kyle's eyes grew wide. "He attacked again? I thought he was being taken care of."

I crossed my arms. "I thought so, too."

"We need to talk to Fletcher," Marek said.

Just then, Fletcher's car pulled up and parked unevenly next to the curb.

He jumped out of the vehicle with a worried expression on his face. "What's wrong? What's happened?"

Marek glanced around. He seemed to decide it wasn't safe to talk out in the open. "Let's get inside."

Fletcher nodded and hurried toward the school, fumbling with his keys as he went. "Everyone's okay?"

Marek looked at me. "Ryn?"

My heart began to slow. "I'm fine. For now."

Fletcher led the way to his classroom. The remaining four of us filed into seats in the front row. He sat behind his desk and crossed his hands.

"Dorian attacked again," Marek stated flatly.

Fletcher pressed his fingers to his eyes, looking positively distressed. "Tell me exactly what happened."

Allie and Kyle leaned in closer.

"Ryn and I were down in the valley. She'd just taken her first flight, and everyone else left. We were going to get started on conjuring essence, but then the demon attacked me from behind."

Fletcher dropped his hands. "Then what happened?"

Marek looked to me for explanation.

"Dorian was standing at the top of the hill," I said. "He flew down to me, and I conjured essence. I thought I might be able to use it on him. But it was just a little bit. I couldn't sustain it. I knew I didn't stand a chance, so I tried to keep him talking to stall. He said…"

Everyone looked at me expectantly.

I took a deep breath. "He said he wants me to join him."

Fletcher furrowed his brow. "Join him?"

My gut twisted when I thought of Dorian's plan.

"He wants me to help him build an army of demons who have my power," I admitted.

"*What?*" Allie asked in shock. "How would that even work?"

"He wants to—" How could I put this into words? "He wants to *breed* with me. He wants our kids to lead a demon army. He says they'd be unstoppable."

Fletcher shook his head like he couldn't believe what he was hearing. "He clearly doesn't understand your powers."

"What do you mean?" I asked.

"The Power of Grace isn't genetic," Fletcher answered.

Relief washed over me. If what Fletcher said was true, Dorian would *have* to give up on me.

"It takes a physical body to manipulate essence," Fletcher explained. "That's why Grace needs someone else to wake her. Originals couldn't just hand their essence over to a mortal, though. It would destroy the mortal. She, however, can send it *through* you. You, Ryn, are a conduit."

My brows shot up. "A con-du-what?"

"A conduit," Fletcher said. "You've been chosen by Grace to reconnect her essence and consciousness with her body and life energy. Once that connection is restored, she'll be able to access the full potential of her essence once again."

I thought about it for a moment.

"So, what you're saying is—" I stared.

"Grace's power isn't yours to keep," Fletcher finished. "Once you restore the connection between Grace's essence and her body, your powers will return to normal—like the rest of ours."

I was stunned by Fletcher's words. I didn't know what to think.

"How'd you get away from him?" Fletcher asked.

"Away from Dorian? I threatened him," I said. "Marek woke up, and he was trying to help. Then Dorian hit him, and I conjured a purple fireball—"

"They're not fireballs," Marek muttered under his breath.

I shot him the evil eye for interrupting. "I told Dorian to go before I changed my mind."

"You shouldn't have let him," Marek said through gritted teeth.

"You think the alternative is better?" My voice rose. "I'm not going to kill someone!"

Reality slammed into me as soon as I said it. *I've already killed before.*

"Not on purpose, anyway," I clarified in a small voice.

Marek turned to Fletcher. "If Ryn's not going to kill him, someone else has to. He's not going to give up."

"We could reason with him," I argued. "We could tell him what Fletcher just said, about how his plan couldn't ever work."

"You think he'd give up?" Marek asked harshly. "If he's not using you to build an army, he'll use you for something else. The demons would rather kill you than let you wake Grace."

Allie cut in. "What about the team of people you have looking for him, Fletcher?"

"Yeah," Marek agreed. "I thought the Davina in Eagle Valley were supposed to have practical experience."

Fletcher sighed. "Unfortunately, some Davina haven't been as cooperative as I would like. I've essentially been looking for him myself. While I've asked the rest of you to keep an eye on Ryn, I've been canvassing the outskirts of town hoping to run into him. But he's on high alert. I haven't been able to get close enough for combat."

"What's everyone else doing?" Marek snarled. "Casey said her dad was out there looking for him."

"Casey's father, along with the others, don't know about Ryn's... talents," Fletcher said. "They know the demon won't come all the way into town, and though they know Ryn is his target, they're confident she's safe. They aren't trying very hard to find him. They don't see him as a threat."

"That's bull!" Kyle yelled.

"Then we have to tell them about her powers," Marek insisted at the same time.

Fletcher held up a hand to get them both to calm down. "We're not telling them. The more people we tell, the more danger we put Ryn in. Yes, we can trust the Davina, but it's not a matter of trust. Rumors will fly. It just takes *one* person to overhear what Ryn is capable of to put her in more danger."

"Tell them he attacked me, too," Marek suggested. "If they know he's not just out for Ryn, then maybe they'll think twice about how dangerous he is."

Allie shifted in her chair and raised her hand apprehensively, waiting for her turn to speak.

Fletcher raised his eyebrows in interest. "Yes, Allie?"

She cleared her throat. "Well, it's just... I agree with

you. Maybe we shouldn't tell the others. But you already have a group of people who *do* understand the situation and can help out. You have us."

Fletcher shook his head with conviction. "No. I don't want to put any of you in more danger. I want all of you to stay in town until I can get this sorted out. No more going to the valley until next week. Without enough people coming and going during school hours, it leaves you too exposed. Ryn, I want you to continue trying to conjure essence but at home instead of the valley. Once we eliminate this threat, we'll have much more time for lessons."

I nodded.

"I know a way we could end this sooner," Kyle said.

We all looked to him in question.

"We use Ryn as bait."

"*What?*" I practically choked.

"No," Marek protested.

"Kyle," Allie said in disbelief.

"Just hear me out," Kyle insisted. "This demon's attacked her twice now at the valley. We go back out there and set up a similar scenario but have people surrounding the valley to attack *him* as soon as he shows."

I couldn't believe what I was hearing. "You can't really think he's that stupid, can you?"

Kyle shrugged. "It's worth a shot. He either shows up and we get him, or he doesn't and no one gets hurt."

"Kyle—" I started, but Fletcher cut me off.

"No. We're not using Ryn as bait. Ryn, I want you to go home and stay there. I'm getting a better feel for this Aedes' movements. I should have him taken care of before school starts."

"Can't we at least do something to *help?*" Marek asked.

Fletcher raised his brows. "Yes. You can keep Ryn company."

"Fine." Marek sounded slightly irritated, like he'd rather be out there with Fletcher than babysitting me. He stood.

"Wait," Kyle insisted. "Can't we talk about this more? The sooner we get rid of this demon, the better."

Marek turned to Kyle with a hard look on his face. "You think I don't know that? I want to get rid of him, too, but Fletcher's right. We have to protect Ryn." He turned to me and softened his voice. "Let's get you somewhere safe for the night."

My heart melted. How'd I manage to find this guy who wanted to protect me at any cost?

Allie, Kyle, and I stood to follow him.

I paused at the door. "Fletcher?"

I could see the apology written all over his face. He obviously felt bad that he hadn't caught Dorian yet.

"I'm really grateful for all your help," I told him. "Thanks for watching out for me."

A smile crept across his face, melting away the disappointment on it. "That's what I'm here for. Please do me a favor, Ryn."

"Yeah?"

"Stay safe, okay?"

I nodded. "I will."

I wasn't sure I'd be able to keep that promise.

We stepped outside into heavy air. The clouds had thickened, darkening the sky.

"What are we supposed to do now?" Kyle asked. "Just sit around and do nothing?"

"I don't know." Marek ran his fingers through his hair.

"I have an idea," I offered. "We could go back to Allie's and you could show me how to conjure fireballs."

Marek frowned at my use of the term *fireballs*.

"If I can learn to conjure white fireballs by will, I'll be able to defend myself without hurting anyone." I stared at Marek pleadingly. He had to know how much I didn't want anyone to get hurt.

We stopped beside Allie's vehicle.

"I'd personally love to see Ryn use the Power of Grace," Kyle said.

"Me, too," Allie agreed. "And Fletcher said he wanted her to keep trying with it."

Marek pursed his lips.

"What?" I asked. "You think it's a bad idea? I won't hurt anyone in a controlled environment."

Marek sighed. "It's not that."

"Then what?" I demanded.

Marek gritted his teeth like he didn't want to say. We all stared back at him expectantly.

He finally caved. "Forget what Fletcher said. I want to go after this demon."

"No!" I objected. The last thing I wanted was for him to get hurt.

"You can't," Allie agreed.

"Calm down, Marek," Kyle said. "You're not going anywhere."

Marek glared at Kyle like he couldn't believe he was giving orders. He ran his fingers through his hair again.

"I know." Marek crossed his arms. "That's why I need someone to talk me out of it."

"Fletcher's taking care of it," Allie said.

Somehow, I didn't think that would convince Marek.

I stepped forward until Marek and I were just inches apart. I stared intensely into his eyes.

"You can't," I said in a near whisper. "Who would protect me if you weren't around?"

Marek's expression softened. He held my gaze for several seconds but didn't say anything.

"Um, hello?" Kyle said. "Allie and I aren't completely useless."

Thanks, Kyle. You just invalidated my entire argument.

Allie elbowed him softly in the ribs.

"Ow!" Kyle elbowed her back.

Marek laughed lightly and relaxed his shoulders. "Ryn's right. I can't leave her alone with you two idiots. Let's go conjure some essence."

~

We spent the next hour in Allie's basement while I tried to conjure what essence I could. No matter how hard I tried, I couldn't manage more than a spark.

Kyle sprawled himself in the bean bag chair in the corner, making comments every now and then about how I was doing it wrong or how I wasn't trying hard enough. Allie told me at least six times to ignore him.

Eventually, my annoyance turned to anger. I tried to let that fuel my power, but it didn't work as I'd hoped. It was only when Kyle turned to criticizing Marek for his teaching methods and no one was paying attention that I felt a surge of electricity pass between my fingertips. As soon as I got their attention, it was gone.

"Stop being a jerk, Kyle," Allie snapped at him.

He spread his arms wide as if to ask what he'd done wrong. "I'm only trying to help motivate."

Allie rolled her eyes. "Yeah, well, you're doing it wrong."

Kyle let out a puff of air and turned his attention to his phone.

"It's okay, Allie," I told her. "I think Kyle may have actually helped a little. So far, it seems to only work for me when I'm angry."

"See?" Kyle said without looking up. "I *was* helping."

"I'm sorry I'm being so slow," I told them.

"It just takes practice," Marek assured me.

"Let me try again." I raised my palm and took a deep breath in concentration.

As the seconds ticked by, the tension in my head intensified. I glared into my hand like I could make it combust by sheer will.

Nothing happened.

I sighed. "Forget it. Maybe I'll do better another time."

"It's fine," Allie assured me sympathetically. "We'll try again tomorrow."

I forced a smile. "Thanks."

"Maybe we should take a break," Marek suggested.

I nodded. "Is it okay if I step outside for some fresh air?" I needed a chance to clear my head after the long day I'd endured.

"Yeah," Marek agreed. "Let's go out back."

I hadn't intended it as an invitation, but after everything that happened, I didn't think any of them would be letting me out of their sight anytime soon.

Allie and Kyle stayed behind as Marek and I climbed the stairs and stepped out into the back yard.

A slight breeze had picked up, chilling my exposed skin. I wrapped my arms around myself and sank into one of the swings on the playset next to the house. The whole thing was rusted and looked like it hadn't been played on in years. Marek sat in the swing beside me and swayed slightly.

I stared down at my feet in the dirt, but I could still feel Marek's gaze on me.

"I'm sorry," I whispered.

"For what?"

I closed my eyes and focused on the wind rustling through my hair. I thought for a moment that turning my attention to something so mundane might help take my mind of things, but the emotions I'd been feeling lately bubbled even closer to the surface. I didn't even know at this point *what* I was feeling, but I knew that most of it wasn't good.

"I don't know." I shrugged. "For being such a wimp. For having to turn to you every time I need my ass saved."

"Hey," he said with a hint of a smile. "Don't be sorry about that. It's what I'm here for."

I shot back a half-smile of my own, but it didn't last long. "I feel so useless. According to Fletcher, I'm some prophesied last hope, but I'm the furthest thing anyone would want to bet on. I might literally cause the end of the world because I won't be able to live up to my calling."

Marek frowned. "You shouldn't feel that way."

I couldn't bring myself to believe him.

"I don't get why *I* have this special power," I said. "It should be you, or Allie, or someone else who actually knows what they're doing."

Marek dug his feet into the dirt, stopping his swaying. "I didn't always know what I was doing."

I glanced his way for a second and then returned to staring at my feet. "You know what you're doing now."

Marek breathed a heavy sigh. "It took me almost a year after moving here before I could use my powers properly. You've already conjured essence a handful of times. It's not going to be long before you learn to control it."

It took him a whole year?

"How'd you learn?" I asked.

He shrugged. "I figured out what was holding me back."

"What was it?" I wondered if it could it be the same thing holding me back.

Marek let out a light laugh. "Me."

I looked at him curiously. "What do you mean by that?"

"*I* was holding me back. I didn't want to be a part of this world. My mom was born into a Davina family, but she didn't have Davina powers."

I remembered Marek said not all Davina developed powers. I hadn't expected him to know one of those Davina.

"When we found out I was a Davina, she wasn't exactly happy about it," he admitted. "When I moved in with my aunt, she tried to explain some of it to me, but Fletcher laid on all the details. It was too much. That's when I ran away."

Shock riveted through me. I definitely wasn't expecting to hear that. But I didn't dare interrupt his story.

"The thing was, I had no money and had nowhere to go," he continued. "I just wanted to get away, to erase my past and start over fresh."

I wanted to ask him about his past; I wondered if it had anything to do with his scars. But I didn't want to intrude on his privacy.

"I didn't realize at the time Eagle Valley *was* my fresh start," Marek said. "I was gone two weeks before they found me. Between walking partway and stowing away the other part, I'd only made it about a hundred miles from here. I was so hungry and tired that I didn't really have any choice but to come back."

My heart broke at his story.

"It took another year before I finally embraced what I was and conjured essence for the first time." He shot me a half-hearted smile that didn't reach his eyes. "So, like I said, you're not doing bad for having just discovered what you are."

We both went silent. I had no idea what to say to him. I wanted to offer him my comfort, but Marek was already so tough. I wasn't sure it would help.

"Why are you telling me all this?" I asked.

Marek looked at me intensely. "Because I want you to know that you're stronger than you think you are."

A blush rose to my cheeks. Could he really mean it?

"Besides," Marek continued, "everyone else at Galen already knows. I'd rather you heard about it from me first."

It was evident in his voice that telling me about his past had been difficult for him.

I twisted my swing toward him. "Thank you for telling me."

Hopefully he knew how much I truly meant it.

"Trust me," he said, "you'll learn eventually. You've only just discovered your powers."

Or so you think.

I bit my lip and avoided his gaze.

"What?" he asked. He clearly knew I was hiding something.

Should I tell him?

"The thing is," I said shyly, "I've conjured essence before."

Okay, I guess I'm telling him.

I twisted my hands in my lap. "I didn't know what had happened at the time, but…"

I went silent.

"But what?" Marek asked.

What if he thinks I'm crazy?

I slowly lifted my gaze until our eyes connected. Marek stared back at me with a look of trustworthiness in his eyes. I couldn't explain the sudden desire to tell him everything.

The words tumbled out of me before I could stop myself.

"Friday night wasn't the first time my essence killed someone."

24

I didn't know what possessed me to tell Marek. I hadn't told anyone before in my life.

"I'm sorry," I said in a breathless whisper.

Is Marek the right person to tell about this?

He leaned closer to me in his swing. His face was so close that I could see the small flecks of brown spotted in his blue irises. "It's okay. You can tell me."

Can I?

"I'm afraid you'll tell me I'm crazy," I admitted.

Marek reached up a hand to tuck a strand of brown hair out of my face. My breath caught in my chest.

"I won't," he promised.

I knew he was telling the truth. And maybe that's why my subconscious decided to toss the confession out there. I'd never told anyone before because I knew they wouldn't believe me. Marek was different.

I took a deep breath. "Growing up and not knowing what I was, I didn't know the demons were dangerous.

Pretty much as soon as I could talk, I started talking to them."

"And?" Marek encouraged me to continue.

"There was one demon in particular who always hung around. Clinton. He'd talk to me and play games with me. My mom would play along, but I could always tell she didn't quite believe that he was real. She'd sometimes say something about my *'imaginary friend.'* I knew she was talking about him because he could talk directly at her and she wouldn't respond. Is that normal for demons? To befriend kids?"

Marek pressed his lips together. "It seems strange. Demons would normally feed off your essence rather than befriend you. You never felt influenced by him?"

I shook my head. "I don't think so."

Then again, who knew what it felt like?

"Maybe it was different because you're a Davina," Marek suggested.

I shrugged. "Knowing what I know now, I wonder if he was more interested in my mom than me. She wasn't in a good place during my childhood."

How much should I tell him?

"Once I was a little older," I said, "I thought it was because she lost my dad. Now I wonder if all that bad stuff was because of Clinton."

"It's pretty normal for humans to have a demon—sometimes even more than one—attached to them," Marek said.

I frowned. "You haven't heard the half of it. Like I said, my mom was in a bad place. She—"

No, I can't tell him.

This wasn't exactly something you tell a guy you just met. At the same time, I wanted the weight lifted off my shoulders. I'd been holding onto this secret for too long.

"She what?" he prodded. "It's safe to tell me. I'm not going to judge."

I took another long breath. "My mom drank a lot."

I was surprised at how good it felt to finally open up to someone.

"The thing was," I continued, "Clinton would always egg her on. I was so young, I didn't realize what was happening. Most of the time, I thought he was joking around. And it seemed harmless, you know? All he was doing was *talking.* Things like *'one more drink'* and *'Kathryn would be better off without you.'*"

Marek's eyes filled with sympathy, but he didn't say anything.

"I guess when I was seven or so, I started to realize how awful he was being," I said. "I'd tell him to stop. I'd tell him he was lying to her. By that time, my mom had already sent me to therapy. She said it was because I should be past my stage of imaginary friends."

My chest knotted. The next part of the story was the hardest.

"Then what happened?" Marek asked softly.

I forced the knot to ease. "One night when I was eight, my mom drank so much she passed out on the couch. I yelled at Clinton and asked him why he encouraged her to drink so much. All he did was laugh at me. That was when I decided I hated him."

The memory of Clinton left a bad taste in my mouth.

"I told him to leave," I continued. "I said I was going to call the cops on him. I mean, I was eight. What else was I supposed to threaten him with? And obviously I wasn't going to do it because at this point, I knew no one else could see him."

Marek nodded like he understood.

"I locked myself in my bedroom," I told him, "but he didn't leave. I couldn't bring myself to fall asleep because I was so mad. Eventually, I heard my mom creep down the hall to her room across from mine. I waited a couple of minutes and decided I wanted to sleep by her that night. Only, when I opened the door—"

An involuntary sob caught in my throat. Marek touched my shoulder lightly.

"It's okay," he said.

I shook my head, unable to choke out the words. It really *wasn't* okay.

Maybe I should stop, I told myself. *I've told him enough.*

Except I wanted to tell him more. Getting it off my chest was a relief. I couldn't stop now.

My breathing wavered. "When I opened the door, he was standing over her… telling her to kill herself."

I couldn't help it as the tears fell down my cheeks and my body shook in sobs. I covered my face with my hands and barely noticed when Marek wrapped an arm around me. I wanted his warm embrace to soothe me, but nothing could help erase the images burned into my memory.

"I just remember so much blood," I cried into his chest.

Marek didn't say a word. He only pulled me closer as we lightly swayed back and forth in the swings.

I didn't know how long we stayed there. When my tears finally dried, I pulled away and wiped at my face.

I swallowed down the lump in my throat. "I saw the cuts on her wrists, and I yelled at Clinton. I told him it was his fault. He told me he knew, that it's what he *wanted*."

Bile rose to my throat at the memory.

"The night my mom tried to kill herself, I used essence on Clinton," I admitted. "I don't really remember it. I just remember this bright purple light shoot across the room, and then he was gone… vanished into thin air."

I paused. "All that was left was his cloak. I never touched it when we moved. Since she's human, my mom never knew it was there in the first place."

Marek took a deep breath beside me like he was going to say something, but he remained silent.

"As soon as Clinton was gone, I called 911 then wrapped my mom's wrists with the blanket on her bed. I saved her life." My voice cracked. "Sometimes, I wonder what would've happened if I hadn't walked in on her, if I had fallen asleep or something."

I couldn't bear to think of that. "I'd spent so long trying to forget that night. All these years, I felt like I was somehow to blame, like Clinton was some sort of omen telling me it was coming…"

I sniffled and wiped at my eyes again. "Mom got better after that. I told her I'd stopped seeing Clinton because, well, it was true. And I pretended like I couldn't see the rest of them. If I acted like I could, I was afraid something bad might happen again. So I ignored them, never made eye contact, never once spoke back to them."

Marek nodded in understanding.

"It was hard at first," I said. "I wanted to be home-schooled to avoid them altogether. But that was right when Mom started working from home so we could move around—and 'see the world,' she said—so she didn't have the time to homeschool me."

She never made the time for me at all, and then she'd act like it was my fault.

I sighed heavily. "I've spent most of my life believing I was imagining it all. That's why I thought I was hallucinating—or drugged—the night we met. I never knew what really happened to Clinton until you told me I'd killed that other demon."

My gaze finally locked on his again. After sharing so much about myself with Marek, all I wanted to do was stare into his eyes. They remained soft, like he really cared about what I was saying.

I wiped at my nose. "I'm sorry about crying."

"Don't be sorry," he said gently, pulling me once again back to his chest. "*I'm* sorry all that happened to you. You have every right to feel upset over it."

I forced a smile, even though he couldn't see it. "Thanks."

Marek loosened his hold on me, and I drew away. He stared down at me.

"What?" I asked shyly.

His eyes danced across my face. "I just want to protect you."

My heart flipped in my chest. "From what?"

"From Clinton. From Dorian. From everything."

"You can't protect me from everything," I told him.

Marek frowned and pulled me back to his chest. His breath was warm against the top of my head.

His words came in a low whisper. "I can try."

25

"Marek! Marek!" I cried.

I glanced around frantically, searching for an indication of where I was and what I was doing there. In front of me spanned a large patch of grass, but beyond that, nothing. A thick layer of gray fog obscured my view.

"Marek!" I called again.

"Ryn?" An unfamiliar voice cut through the fog.

"Who's there?" I demanded.

"It's me," the voice said.

A figure stepped forward. It was a young man who looked to be about thirteen. He stood shirtless and shaking in front of me. White wings rose behind him, giving him away as Davina. His blue eyes looked familiar, but I couldn't place him.

"Are you okay?" I asked, quickly rushing to the boy.

His bottom lip quivered, and his eyes filled with terror. "Ryn, I need your help."

"It's okay," I told him, but I couldn't be sure without knowing what was actually wrong.

181

A woman's voice echoed from somewhere past the fog. "I will NOT raise a Davina. You are a disgrace!"

I surveyed the area in a heartbeat, searching for the woman the voice belonged to, but I saw nothing. When I glanced back to where the boy stood, he was gone. Instead, Marek stood in his place, complete with his leather jacket and a hard look on his face.

"We shouldn't be here, Ryn," he said, stepping forward to take me by the elbow.

I dug my feet into the grass and pulled away. "We have to save the boy!"

He reached for me again. "We can't, Ryn."

Marek's grip was so tight that I couldn't pull away this time. He dragged me alongside him.

"Why not?" I insisted.

"Because, Ryn, he's already gone."

"But Marek!" I jerked away again.

"Come on, Ryn," he insisted. "We have to go. He'll be here soon!"

"The boy? He was just here."

"No, not him."

"Then who?"

Laughter echoed around me, but I couldn't tell where it was coming from. As the eerie sound intensified, the fog began to clear. A hill rose in the distance, and I noticed for the first time I was standing at the base of the valley. I could just barely make out a dark figure with massive black wings at the top of the hill.

"Dorian?" I turned back to Marek for confirmation, but he was gone.

Panic entered my chest. How could he just abandon me?

I heard the flapping of wings and turned my full attention back to Dorian. By now, the fog had completely lifted, but the atmosphere remained a grayish tint that sent a chill down my spine.

With every increasingly rapid breath, Dorian got closer to me. I should've run, but I stood my ground.

"You can't win this fight, Dorian!" I shouted.

A dark fireball had already settled in his palm when he landed.

"That's where you're wrong." He didn't waste another second as he hurled the fireball toward me.

Instinct overcame me, and I jumped to dodge it. I expected my feet to hit the ground a moment later, but I was surprised to find myself airborne. A strong wind passed by my face. I flapped my wings harder, rising above Dorian.

He threw another fireball.

I dodged that one as well as the next.

I landed gracefully beside him. "This is a war you can't win, Dorian."

"Of course I can," he said, that cold laugh returning. "You may be the chosen one, but there's just one problem."

I swallowed, not sure if I wanted him to elaborate. My curiosity got the better of me. "What's that?"

Dorian's laughter stopped dead. "They chose wrong."

Then he hurled the essence in his hand at my chest, and everything went dark.

～

I awoke suddenly. My heart raced, and my body was covered in a sheen of sweat. The side of my face stuck to the arm of a leather couch, and a TV played quietly in the background. It took me a moment to remember where I was.

After Marek and I came inside, Allie had put on a movie in the living room. I'd fallen asleep next to Marek. Now I lay alone on the couch with a blanket draped over me that hadn't been there earlier.

I tried to hold onto the memory of my dream, but it was slipping away quickly. Who was that boy I'd dreamt about? He reminded me so much of someone… of Marek.

I realized it as soon as I asked myself the question. He'd been a younger version of Marek, the version who'd run away from Eagle Valley. The woman's voice had been his mother's.

I continued to play the dream back through my mind until I recalled how it ended. Could Nightmare Dorian have been right? Did Grace choose the wrong person?

I looked to Allie and Kyle in the loveseat beside me. Allie lay against Kyle's chest with his arm around her shoulder.

I sat up. "How long was I out?"

Allie shrugged. "Half an hour or so."

"That's it?" I asked in shock. "Where's Marek?"

"He went home a few minutes ago," Allie said.

My heart dropped. It was already dark out, but he could've stayed longer.

"Are you hungry?" Allie asked. "My dad left some chili on the stove. We didn't want to wake you."

"Thanks." I stood.

Allie hopped up from the loveseat to join me in the kitchen. "Do you remember where the bowls and spoons are?"

"Yeah." I helped myself to the silverware.

Allie pulled a bowl down from the cupboard and handed it to me. I ladled chili into my bowl and leaned my hip against the counter to eat.

"So, you and Marek were outside for a while." Allie wiggled her eyebrows. "Anything fun happen?"

I rolled my eyes at her. "Could you at least give us a month to get to know each other?"

"A whole *month*?" she teased, sticking her bottom lip out. "You never let me have any fun."

I swallowed my chili and laughed.

Allie pulled a clean glass from the drying rack and began filling it at the sink. "No, but seriously. I saw you two hugging."

I rose my eyebrows at her. "And what were you doing spying on us?"

Allie's eyes widened innocently. "I wasn't! You can see the swing set from the window." She gestured to the window above the sink.

I glanced outside. I could just barely make out the silhouette of the swing set through the darkness. Lightning lit up the clouds in the distance.

Allie sipped on her water. "What'd you two talk about?"

I shrugged. I knew I could tell Allie about Clinton because she was a Davina, but telling the story once today was enough.

I stared out the window. "Marek was just telling me I wasn't doing so bad. He told me he ran away when he came here."

Allie frowned. "Yeah, he did."

Another bolt of lightning lit up the sky. The thick cloud cover diffused the light.

"Who did what?" Kyle stepped into the room.

"Marek ran away," Allie said simply, taking another gulp of water.

Kyle crossed his arms in amusement and leaned against the counter. "Oh, that story."

I barely processed what they were saying. My attention remained locked on the lightning in the distance. Something was *off* about it.

And then I saw it.

A light shot up into the sky, illuminating the clouds. As fast as the flash came, it was gone.

"What are you looking at?" Allie followed my gaze toward the horizon.

I set my bowl on the counter, never taking my eyes off the night sky. "Is it just me, or is there something strange about that lightning?"

Kyle joined us at the window to get a good look. The light shot into the sky again and flashed through the clouds. Kyle let out a breath in disbelief. Allie and I looked at him for explanation. He twisted his lips and shook his head.

"That son of a bitch," he said in amusement.

"What do you mean?" I asked.

Kyle laughed lightly. "That's not lightning."

Allie drew in a breath of surprise. Clearly she understood something I didn't.

"If it's not lightning—" I stopped dead.

We were in Eagle Valley. What else could it be?

"Essence?" I asked.

Kyle nodded.

"I thought that was supposed to be kept secret," I said.

Allie frowned. "It is."

"Then why's someone out there doing that?" I asked.

Kyle scoffed. "Isn't it obvious?"

No, you dimwit. I'm not exactly familiar with this Davina stuff.

I shook my head.

Kyle smiled in amusement. "I'd bet you anything it's your boyfriend out there. He's going after the demon himself."

26

"He can't!" I cried. My eyes widened in shock. Kyle shrugged. "He did."

"How do you know it's him?" I demanded.

"Because it's something he would do," Allie answered with an eye roll.

Kyle gestured out the window. "And check out where it's coming from."

I considered it for a moment. "The valley."

Kyle nodded.

"We have to go!" I was already on my way to the back door. Marek wasn't going to get hurt because of me.

"Hold on," Allie called. "Ryn!"

I raced through Allie's back yard and across the neighbor's.

"Marek's such an idiot," Allie mumbled from several paces back.

That, or my hero. We have yet to find out.

Kyle and Allie caught up to me when I reached the sidewalk, but I didn't slow my pace. I sprinted as fast as I could in the direction of Galen High.

My legs burned as we neared the school. It felt like a weight had settled on my chest as I sucked in shallow breaths. But it never felt like I was getting enough oxygen.

I definitely needed to pick up running. And maybe cut back on the cookies.

The three of us ran around the side of the school. We increased our speed as soon as we hit the trail. Through the trees, I saw Marek's essence shoot upward and illuminate the sky again. What was he thinking?

As we raced closer, I heard his voice cut through the sound of the wind.

"Come on!" he shouted. There was a raw passion in his voice I'd never heard before. "I know you're out there."

I broke through the trees and came to a sudden halt next to Marek's bike. Allie stumbled into me but caught herself on my shoulder. Kyle stopped beside her.

Below us, Marek stood in the center of the valley. Another fireball was ready in his hand, illuminating him. He paced back and forth aggressively with his head tilted toward the sky.

"Where are you, you jackass?" he roared. "Come fight me. Let's see who really deserves her!"

Marek closed his fist, and the fireball inside it disappeared. Darkness enveloped the valley. The next moment, a white fireball erupted from his palm and shot straight into the sky like a firework. It reached the low-hanging clouds. They lit for less than a second before the valley became dark again.

"Marek, stop!" I called from the top of the hill.

I hardly thought about it when I flexed my shoulders and wings grew out of my back. I threw my body forward and spread my wings out.

Marek conjured another fireball to illuminate his face. He looked in my direction as I descended toward him. I could hear Allie's and Kyle's wings flapping behind me.

I aimed for landing next to him, but I hadn't perfected my landing yet. I stumbled into him and caught myself on the sleeve of his jacket.

The fireball in his hand disappeared. He grabbed my arms to steady me, but the valley didn't go dark. I glanced behind me to see that Allie and Kyle were holding fireballs of their own.

Marek gripped my biceps hard and forced me to look at him. "You shouldn't be here."

"*You* shouldn't be here," I accused. "What were you thinking?"

His eyes searched mine, but his voice remained strong. "I was thinking I wanted to protect you."

"But Fletcher said—" I started.

"Forget what Fletcher said," Marek growled. "You need to get out of here. All of you."

"We're not going anywhere without you," I stated confidently.

"Please," Marek pleaded. "You weren't supposed to follow me. If he got my message, he's almost here."

Kyle stepped forward. "Marek, you're being an idiot."

Thank God someone agreed with me.

"You're not going to talk me out of it," Marek declared.

"I know," Kyle said. "You're too stubborn for that. The least you can do is let us fight alongside you."

Apparently Kyle wasn't taking my side after all.

Jerk.

"No." Marek's voice was strong and commanding. "Not Ryn. I left her with you so you could protect her."

Kyle frowned. "Then you should've told me your plan."

Allie stepped between them. "You're both being ridiculous. Fletcher is taking care of this demon. We need to get out of here before—"

An explosion like a firecracker at our feet cut her off. Every muscle in my body contracted.

It took me only a moment of confusion to realize what it'd been.

Essence.

A warning.

I whirled around quickly. What I saw sent my heart tumbling out of my chest.

A dark winged figure I recognized all too well swooped out of the sky and landed just yards away from us.

If at any moment I'd felt hopeless in all my encounters with Dorian, it was nothing compared to how I felt when six other cloaked figures soared out of the shadows behind him.

27

Seven demons surrounded us.

A dark fireball with its red and white outline glowed in Dorian's palm and illuminated the bottom half of his thin face. Fear instinctively hit, but it was quickly overshadowed by anger when I noticed his smirk.

He's not going to win.

Marek grabbed my wrist and pulled me behind him.

Allie and Kyle stood facing the circle of demons with their backs toward me. I was enclosed in a protective triangle between the three of them. Allie's and Kyle's wings helped hide me.

I stared past Marek to Dorian. "I thought you wanted all the glory for yourself."

Marek pushed me further behind him.

Dorian grinned. "I told you I wasn't going to give you a choice."

"Didn't think you could take me on alone, did you?" I taunted.

"Don't worry," Dorian said with a laugh. "You're still mine. I only recruited a few people to take care of your friends."

Dorian reached up with one hand to lower his hood. He looked mostly human, but there was something evil about him that made my stomach twist. His eyes held that same darkness in them I'd noticed before. This time, it was even more apparent and terrifying.

"Sorry to disappoint," I said, "but you've recruited for nothing. There's nothing you can do to make me go with you."

"Quiet," Marek hissed. He scanned the circle of demons like he was calculating how to take them all out.

"I wouldn't be so sure about that," Dorian mocked. "I'm giving you one last chance to join me. If you refuse, you can say goodbye to your friends."

Someone might as well have dropped a cinderblock on my stomach. We were outnumbered. If I didn't go with him, my friends were going to die.

There has to be a way out of this.

"Your plan will never work," Marek snarled. "The demons will never have the Power of Grace."

"Shut up, Lover Boy," Dorian barked.

"It's true!" Allie cried. She never took her eyes off the other demons. "Her power isn't genetic."

"You're lying!" Dorian accused.

"She's not," Kyle defended.

Marek stepped further in front of me for protection. I couldn't see Dorian's reaction.

After a few moments, Dorian spoke again. "Doesn't matter either way. Her power is too unique."

And he wants every bit of it for himself.

My chest tightened. Marek's words echoed in my head.

If he's not using you to build an army, he'll use you for something else.

Marek squeezed my hand. "If you want her, you'll have to come through us to get her."

Dorian scoffed. "If that's how you want to do this…"

Everyone moved in a blur. The six other demons closed in on us, and my friends immediately sprang into action. Marek's hold on me vanished as he aimed a punch at the closest demon.

Before I could make a move, Dorian had closed the distance between us and had me in his grasp. He spun me around and held me to his chest, pinning my wings at an awkward angle between us.

I watched in horror as a demon sank a foot into Marek's abdomen. Marek conjured a fireball. Nearby, Allie threw a kick into a demon's gut and elbowed another in the face. Kyle tackled one to the ground and smashed his fist into its face over and over again.

Dorian's cold breath across my cheek sent a chill down my spine. "Are you ready to come with me now?"

I squirmed. "I'll never go with you."

Dorian clicked his tongue. "Not the answer I wanted to hear, Little Angel. Though, your resistance is a bit of a turn-on." Dorian pressed his hips into my backside and trailed a hand down my stomach to my waistline.

I gritted my teeth.

"Stop!" I demanded.

"Stop what?" he taunted. "Stop my friends from killing yours? Or stop this?" His fingers slid across my hip.

"Please," I cried.

How had this happened? How had I let him get me in this position again?

Dorian squeezed me tighter. "That's it, my Little Angel. Beg for it."

My breath grew hot on my upper lip. "I. Am. Not. Your. Little. Angel."

A strength I didn't know I had overcame me. I lifted my foot and slammed it down hard on his toes. His grip on me loosened, and I took the opportunity to swing my elbow up into his nose. He stumbled back and released me.

I raced away from him as fast as my legs could carry me and launched myself into the air. A ball of black magic flew by my head, narrowly missing my shoulder. I didn't look back, but I knew Dorian was flying close behind me.

I'm going to die. Just like in my dream.

I somehow missed another one of Dorian's attacks. I was quickly reaching the end of the valley and didn't know how much longer I could hold him off. Any moment, he could knock me out of the air.

Don't let him get to you, I told myself.

Instantly, I knew the only thing I could do was hide. I didn't worry about landing gracefully. My only mission was to get into the trees—and *fast*. At least in there, I had some cover.

I landed hard at the top of the valley opposite the trail we normally came in on. I stumbled to my knees but quickly got to my feet and took off running. I pulled my wings into me so they wouldn't slow me down.

Rather than dodging Dorian's attacks, I found myself dodging around trees and jumping over thick roots. There was no path here, and the forest was denser than I thought it would be.

My hand scraped along the bark of the trees as I passed each one. I used their sturdy trunks to help me stay upright. Just as my hand found another tree, a dark fireball passed through it and fizzled out just feet ahead of me. I didn't let my shock slow me down. I was immediately on to the next tree, still jumping over roots and fallen sticks as fast as I could.

As another fireball rushed by my head, I knew Dorian couldn't be far behind. I gave up using the trees as support and let my legs carry me through the thick forest. I concentrated as much as I could to get that white fireball to appear in my fist.

Nothing came, not even a tingle.

How had this worked every other time fear overcame me, but it wasn't working now when I needed it the most?

Not fear, I reminded myself. *Anger.*

I dodged around another tree and shifted course to the left, hoping to confuse Dorian even if it only put him another second behind me.

My body continued to move forward, but my mind focused on all the things I could possibly think to be angry about.

I was angry at my mom for making us move every year, even though I pretended like I was fine with it. I was angry at Allie for acting like being a Davina was so easy. I was angry at Marek for trying to face Dorian on his own instead of letting Fletcher take care of it.

I was angry at Grace for choosing *me* and expecting me to do something with her powers when I had no clue, at my father for abandoning me and never coming back to explain any of it, at Clinton for all he did to my mom and our family, and at Fletcher for expecting so much from me.

My skin heated, and not just from running. All these thoughts bubbled to the surface. I thought for a moment that I might have to stop running to let myself puke.

You can't stop. Dorian isn't far behind.

I focused my anger on Dorian. If I had anything to be angry about, it was the sadistic pig on my tail. All the anger I felt sent me sprinting forward even faster.

I glanced behind me to see Dorian's body pass through the nearest tree like he was a ghost. With the curse keeping him from interacting with this realm, the trees weren't an obstacle for him.

He lunged for me. His solid body slammed into me, knocking me into a thick tree. Dorian fell to the ground. My shoulder ached from the impact, but I quickly recovered and continued running.

A distant scream reached my ears.

Dammit. My friends were still in danger, and I'd abandoned them.

I switched course again. My lungs grew heavy from the sprint. Ahead, a dull glow from the town's light pollution broke through the dense canopy. I'd circled around and was almost back to the valley. I sprinted out of the trees, tensed my shoulders, and hurled my body into the air.

Over my own labored breathing and the rush of air around my ears, I just barely caught the sound of battle below me. Grunts, screams, and the occasional firecracker pop of exploding essence echoed throughout the valley.

"No one's going to save you," Dorian shouted.

He was close. Too close.

He was also wrong.

A white-winged Davina flew high above the valley, surveying the area. Marek immediately dove for us with a white fireball ready in his palm. He hurled it at Dorian, but it only caught him in the ankle. Dorian faltered for a moment, but it wasn't enough to knock him out of the sky.

Below us, five demons remained, looking like nothing more than shadows in the night.

I noticed an extra pair of white wings. Another Davina had come to join the fight. He smashed a fist into the closest demon, sending him stumbling to the ground.

Beside them, Kyle raised his arm toward a nearby demon. A dagger glistened in his hand, reflecting the light from his essence in his other palm. He slashed downward, and the dagger sank into the demon's chest. Death was immediate, and the demon vanished from the valley.

The wind picked up, throwing off my balance in the sky. My wings began to tire as I wove a random path to keep from becoming an easy target.

Come on, Marek, I begged silently. *Knock him out of the sky already.*

The sound of Dorian's flapping wings grew closer.

Allie let out a scream.

My heart stopped in my chest when I saw a demon had knocked her to the ground and kicked her hard in the abdomen. He rose his foot above her face.

"No!" I cried. I immediately dove toward the demon.

I closed in on him fast, but before I made it, something struck my right wing. My wing seized up, paralyzed. I spiraled the remaining fifteen feet out of the sky and collided with the demon. The wind left my chest, and we skidded across the dirt.

I instinctively pulled my wings into me and quickly got to my feet before air returned to my lungs.

The first thing I noticed was the new Davina fighting a demon beside me. He was older, with graying white hair. His bare torso was toned, and he wore his regular tan slacks.

Fletcher.

I didn't have more than a split second to consider his presence. Dorian swooped down out of the sky with another ball of essence ready. I realized immediately that's what had struck my wing, though it hadn't been enough to knock me out. I threw myself to the grass, ducking out of the way of his next attack. Dorian continued flying with Marek still close on his tail.

Out of the corner of my eye, I caught the moment when Kyle raised his dagger to another demon. The demon lunged for him and seized his wrist. Kyle stumbled back but resisted against the demon's hold. The demon's elbow connected with Kyle's face. He snatched the dagger from his grasp and slashed it in Kyle's direction. Kyle dodged out of the way.

I scurried to my feet and rushed toward Kyle to offer my aid.

Allie made it to him first. Her weight crashed into the demon, but she wasn't strong enough to knock him off his feet. The demon grabbed ahold of her and pinned her to his chest. The blade he held pressed into her throat.

I stopped dead in my tracks as time slowed down. It felt as though someone had swung a baseball bat at my gut. Blood pulsed loudly in my ears, drowning out all other sounds.

I couldn't hear Marek above me shouting obscenities at Dorian. I never heard the *pop* of the fireball that exploded against Fletcher's shoulder and knocked him out. I never heard Kyle's body hit the ground as a demon tackled him and pinned his throat beneath his hands.

All I knew was that my best friend was about to die and there was nothing I could do to save her in the split second it would take the demon to slit her throat.

A panicked shriek ripped out of my lungs. "STOP!"

The valley went dead silent.

28

Electricity sizzled in my palm. A vibrant purple glow illuminated everything nearby—the grass, the demons, Allie.

A moment of clarity struck. I suddenly realized what had been holding me back all this time, why the Power of Grace only appeared intermittently.

Now was the time to use it to my advantage.

I raised my right palm threateningly at the demon holding the blade to Allie's neck. "Let. Her. Go."

Dorian's laughter reached my ears. I turned to find him standing just yards away with his head held high in confidence. His hand tangled in Marek's hair.

Marek's head tilted back, and he grimaced in pain.

Each remaining demon had ahold of one of my friends. I was the last one standing.

My knees shook. There was no way I could take them all on at once.

Dorian smiled in amusement. "Finally. You've been holding out on us, Little Angel."

That son of a bitch needed to stop calling me that.

My jaw tensed. "Let my friends go."

Dorian clicked his tongue and shook his head. "I'm afraid I can't do that. I told you this would happen."

It couldn't. I wouldn't let my friends die.

"How do you expect this to work out?" I demanded. "You have no power in this realm."

An evil grin spread across Dorian's face. "That's not true. Look around you. Who's in the position of power here? *I* call the shots now."

I swallowed the lump in my throat. I couldn't see a way out of this without my friends getting hurt.

"Isaac," Dorian called in a commanding voice. He gestured to the demon pinning Allie to his chest. "Over here."

Dorian forced Marek to his knees beside an unconscious Fletcher.

"Hands on your head," he commanded. "Or Isaac will slit the girl's throat."

Marek did as he was told.

Dorian snatched up a cloak left behind by one of his fallen comrades and tore off a piece of fabric. He forced Marek's hands behind his back and began tying them together with it.

Fletcher stirred on the ground.

One of the demons grabbed him by the neck and forced him to kneel beside Marek. He followed Dorian's example and tied him up.

Fletcher raised his eyes to mine. He had apology written all over his face.

The remaining two demons brought their hostages over and restrained them.

My hand with the fireball inside of it shook. "Please don't do this."

Dorian held his hand out to Isaac, who placed the blade inside it.

Dorian turned toward me with a hard look on his face. "I want you to watch as the life drains from each one of your friends' eyes. It's important that you know *this* is what happens to people who don't follow my orders."

He began pacing in front of the line of Davina kneeling at his feet. "Let's see... which one should we start with? The mentor, the boyfriend, the best friend, or..." His lips curled into a smile, and he pointed the dagger toward Kyle. "What's this one to you?"

"He's my friend!" I cried. "And I swear to God, if you touch one hair on his head—"

"What?" Dorian asked in amusement. "You'll use your powers to kill me? Honey, you've had every chance to knock me down, and so far you've failed to do so. Why is that?"

I hesitated. The purple fireball continued to glow in my palm, and I still couldn't bring myself to use it.

Because I won't stoop to your level.

"It's because you're *weak*," he barked.

"Then what do you want with me?" I snapped.

Dorian smirked. "You may be weak now, but you have

potential. You just need a little direction, a little… motivation."

Dorian made a quick decision on his target and grabbed Allie.

"Stop! I'll go with you." The words shot out of my mouth before I consciously made the decision.

"NO!" Allie and Marek cried together.

"You can't do this, Ryn," Fletcher warned.

Dorian paused with the blade to Allie's throat. "You mean it?"

I didn't have any other choice. Even if I wanted to kill Dorian, my friends would immediately die at the hands of his recruits.

Allie stared at me intensely and shook her head the smallest bit.

The purple essence in my palm fizzled away. "Yes. I'll do whatever you want. Just don't hurt her."

"Good girl." Dorian released his grip on Allie and took a step toward me.

"Don't go with him, Ryn," Marek objected. "We're not worth it."

My eyes fell upon each one of them. In the past few days, they'd shown me a world that didn't just accept my insanity; they shared it with me. Marek had saved my life more than once. He was definitely worth it. All of them were.

"I'm sorry, Marek," I whispered. "You were right. There's no reasoning with him."

I stepped forward to accept my fate.

"Ryn, stop!" Marek insisted.

A demon kicked him in the head from behind. His face smashed into the dirt.

I drew in an involuntary breath. I made a move toward him but stopped myself when the demon raised his foot again. If I tried to save him, they'd only hurt him more.

"You can't go with him," Fletcher said. "Don't worry about us."

Marek lifted his head. "He's right, Ryn. The Davina need you!"

The demon kicked him in the gut, and he cried out in pain.

Kyle cringed beside him, and Allie let out a sob.

I glared at Dorian in horror. "Make him stop! I'm going with you. Let my friends go!"

Dorian grabbed my wrist tightly and pulled me toward him possessively. "I said I wouldn't kill them if you came with me. I never said I wouldn't hurt them."

Marek swung his leg around and knocked the closest demon off his feet. He tried to stand, but a second demon was on top of him a moment later, forcing his face into the dirt.

"Here, Isaac." Dorian held the handle of the blade out toward his friend. "Have fun."

Isaac took the blade. He bent beside Marek and pulled his head back by his hair. He laughed as he ran the blade across the side of Marek's face without breaking skin.

They're going to torture him. All of them.

"NO!" I screamed. "You can't do this!"

Dorian wrapped an arm around my waist and began dragging me away.

"Stop!" I kicked my feet out, but Dorian only squeezed tighter.

Suddenly, every muscle in my body contracted. An electric tingle began in my toes. With each inch it traveled up my body, the sensation intensified. Purple energy danced across the surface of my skin, lighting up my entire body like I was made of mystical lightning.

The demons beside Marek shot to their feet in alarm.

The energy grew in my chest, building exponentially each second until the feeling was so strong I couldn't breathe.

Dorian must've released me, but I never noticed. Every inch of my body was being crushed by an unseen force. I urged to cry out in pain, but I couldn't find my voice. In that moment, I thought for sure the energy would break me.

The next, the Power of Grace burst from my chest. A crack like thunder reverberated around me, and a purple energy wave rapidly swept across the valley in all directions. It blasted the standing demons backward in a single heartbeat.

The pain instantly subsided, and a numbness took over. I could no longer feel my limbs. Without warning, my body crumbled to the ground.

Real thunder roared above me. The first of the heavy raindrops hit my face a moment before the world completely faded away.

29

a bright light shone above me when I opened my eyes. I blinked the world into focus and saw I was lying in an unfamiliar bed. A door stood beyond a half-closed curtain to my right. Sunlight filtered through the window, casting a yellow ray across the tile floor.

My eyes continued to scan the hospital room until they fell upon my mother seated at my bedside. She stared down at the yarn she was twisting into knots. The afghan she was working on nearly touched the floor.

I cleared my throat.

Her eyes instantly met mine. "Kathryn."

She sounded surprised to see me awake. She quickly set her crocheting supplies aside and leaned forward to take my hand.

"How are you feeling?" she asked.

I carefully considered the question. I wasn't in pain, but I felt exhausted and hungry.

"I'm okay," I said in a scratchy voice. "What happened?"

I ran the events of the past few days back through my head. Had it all been a vivid dream I'd made up while in a coma?

Mom handed me a water bottle from the small table beside my bed. "Your friends said you passed out."

My friends? So it *had* been real.

"The doctors ran some tests," she told me. "They were worried about your heart when we brought you in, but your vitals have normalized since then. They wanted to keep you overnight for observation. They have no idea what happened."

And they never will.

I took a greedy gulp of water.

"Where are my friends?" I demanded.

Had they all gotten away from the demons safely?

"They went home last night. I said I'd let them know when you woke up."

"I want to see them." I didn't even give it a second thought.

"Let's wait a bit," she suggested. "We'll have the nurses check you again now that you're awake."

I would've much rather jumped out the window and flown back to Eagle Valley to check on my friends.

Mom pressed the nurse's call button.

I glanced around the room in search of my phone, but it wasn't on the table beside me or anywhere else within view. I didn't see my clothes anywhere, either. I wore nothing but a hospital gown.

"Where's all my stuff?" I sat up in bed, panicked.

Mom stood over me. "Calm down. It's all in a bag right there."

My eyes followed hers to see a plastic bag next to her chair with my clothes in it.

"Give me my phone," I insisted. "I need to call Allie."

"After the nurses take a look at you," Mom insisted.

I huffed and fell onto my back in the bed.

A nurse walked into the room. While she was checking my vitals, I turned back to my mom.

"You saw Allie last night?" I asked. "She's all right?"

My mom sat back in her chair. "Of course she is. Is there any reason she shouldn't be?"

I ignored the question. "Who else was with her?"

"Her boyfriend and that guy with the bike," she answered.

I didn't bother correcting her that Kyle wasn't Allie's boyfriend.

Mom frowned. "I really wished you would've told me where you were going. I said you could stay the night at Allie's, not wander around town at all hours of the night."

Of course. I was lying in a hospital bed and she still found something to chew me out about. I thought back to my car accident not even a year ago. This reminded me so much of that. Mom acted like she cared in the moment, but by the time I'd left the hospital, nothing had changed.

The nurse removed the blood pressure cuff from my arm. "Everything looks good for now. We'll get your doctor in here shortly." She smiled and left the room.

"You're lucky Mr. Fletcher was working late," Mom said.

"What do you mean?"

"You don't remember where you passed out? It was right in front of the school. One of your friends rushed to find help. Another called 911. Your advisor helped keep everything under control. I'm just glad there was an adult around."

"*My* advisor?" I couldn't help but notice her strange choice of words.

Mom tried to hide a smile. "Yes, I signed the paperwork. You're going to Galen High this year."

"Are you serious?" I squeaked, shooting upright in bed.

Mom surrendered to the smile. "Yes."

I sprang out of bed and threw my arms around her neck. "Thank you!"

Maybe something *had* changed between us this time.

My friends arrived an hour later. The doctor hadn't come to check on me yet. I guess when you're not dying, you don't get the expedited hospital discharge procedure.

I convinced Mom she should visit the craft store while we were nearby and that I'd be fine without her. I needed the privacy.

Allie rushed into the room and pulled me into a hug. "How are you?"

I shrugged. "A little weak, but I'll survive."

My eyes traveled past Kyle and Fletcher to land on Marek. His face was covered in bruises, but they already looked a few days old thanks to his fast healing abilities.

Marek stared at me like I was the only person in the room. He stood still for several long seconds, holding my gaze. Then, like he couldn't hold back any longer, he closed the distance between us in two long strides and bent to place a kiss on my forehead.

My heart danced in my chest.

Marek pressed his forehead to mine. "I'm so glad you're okay," he whispered. "Don't ever do something like that again."

It took me a moment to recover from his sudden display of affection.

I pulled away from him. "What do you mean?"

"Sacrificing yourself for the rest of us," he said. "Dorian was bluffing, Ryn. He didn't have the power to get you on his side; you're so much stronger than him. He was playing off your loyalty. Every move he made was meant to scare you."

I let out a breath in disbelief. "And you couldn't have pointed that out to me sooner?" I swatted at him.

He caught my wrist and laughed lightly.

I glanced toward everyone else. "You're all okay, then?"

Allie sat in the chair beside my bed. "We're all fine. It's *you* we're worried about."

"Don't be," I insisted. "Just tell me what happened. Did Dorian get away?"

Fletcher stuck his hands in his pockets and stepped forward. He gazed down at his feet like he was about to deliver bad news.

"What?" I asked in alarm. "What happened?"

"I know you dislike the idea of killing the Aedes,"

Fletcher said, "even if it's what Davina do, but it had to be done."

"You killed them?" I asked. "How? They had you all tied up."

Fletcher shook his head. "No, Ryn. *You* killed them."

Confusion struck. Had I heard him properly?

I furrowed my brow. "No, I didn't."

At least, I didn't remember.

Marek took my hand and nodded. "You used the Power of Grace."

My eyes widened. "That explosion that came from me… it killed them?"

"Yes," Fletcher confirmed. "It almost killed you, too."

I was struck silent, trying to make sense of it all.

Finally, I spoke. "How'd it kill the demons and not the rest of you?"

"We were lucky," Kyle said.

"It was a matter of circumstance," Fletcher explained. "The power came from your heart. It expanded at chest-level and missed those of us on the ground."

I suddenly realized how close I'd come to killing my friends. If the demons hadn't forced them to their knees, they'd be dead, too.

I dropped my gaze to my hands. "I didn't mean to kill anyone."

Marek squeezed my hand tighter. "No one's judging you, Ryn. You did what had to be done. Any other Davina would've done the same."

I looked up at him. "But I didn't know what I was doing."

"Perhaps that's what allowed you to summon so much power," Fletcher suggested. "It was never your intention to kill. It was your intention to save."

I considered Fletcher's words. I'd done what I had to in order to save them.

"Maybe the power came because I discovered the secret to unlocking it," I suggested.

Fletcher raised his eyebrows. The other three leaned in closer.

"I thought I conjured essence when I was angry," I told them. "But I was *really* angry when I was running through the woods, and I still couldn't manage to defend myself. It was only when that demon attacked Allie that anything actually happened. This whole time, that's been the key. I've only conjured essence when I was trying to *protect* someone."

I thought about the first time I'd conjured essence when I was eight. It was because Clinton was a danger to my mother.

"The first time at the party, I was defending Allie from that douche bag Tad," I pointed out. "That same night, I was defending Marek from the demon I killed. When we were practicing, I only felt a spark when Kyle was going off at Marek about stuff. See? I've only been making it work when I thought one of my friends was in danger."

"Hey," Kyle said defensively. "I wasn't putting Marek in danger."

"You were still being a dick," Marek accused.

Kyle shrugged like he couldn't argue with that.

"It's an interesting theory," Fletcher mused.

I stretched my hand out in front of me. "I think now that I know what was holding me back, I may be able to break through this."

I concentrated hard on my palm, flexing my muscles and picturing a white fireball.

Allie drew in a breath beside me.

A white orb rose from my palm. It wasn't the powerful purple it had been when we were fighting, but it was *progress*. I smiled involuntarily and then closed my palm. It disappeared in my fist.

I looked back at Fletcher. "I still have so many questions. How'd you end up fighting with us?"

Allie laughed and shot a glance at Marek. "Same way we did. Marek's fireworks display."

Marek scowled at her.

Fletcher nodded. "I was out in search of signs of the Aedes when I saw James's light show. I thought it was lightning at first."

"Yeah, so did we," I said. "I'm also curious about the knife. How'd it work on the demons?"

"It's a Davina Blade," Fletcher answered.

I remembered he had mentioned them before, about how they came from the Davina realm and were one of their only weapons.

"You had one this whole time?" I asked.

Kyle smirked beside him. "It was my dad's. He was a Protector. And a damn good one."

Fletcher nodded. "I knew him. Your family should've returned that blade after your father's death. Someone's surely wondering why the Protectors are a blade short."

"It was my *dad's*," Kyle bit harshly. "Besides, it came in quite handy. You're not going to make me return it to the Protectors, are you?"

Fletcher fell silent for a moment while considering the question. "No. I think we may want to keep it for now."

"Good. Because I'm not giving it back," Kyle said.

I took a deep breath. "What happened to me afterward?"

"I told you before that the power of an Original is too much for a mortal body to handle," Fletcher explained. "You accessed too much at once. You went into cardiac arrest."

I gasped. "Oh my God. How did I—?"

"Marek," Kyle answered. "Marek saved you."

I looked up at Marek.

He nodded slightly. "I used the blade to cut the fabric off my wrists. I gave you CPR until the medics showed up."

Tears of gratitude rose to my eyes.

"Thank you," I whispered.

He shook his head lightly. "You don't have to thank me."

I didn't care what Marek said. To me, he was truly an angel.

"Why are you stopping?" I asked.

Marek slowed his bike outside of town the next day. He parked along the shoulder of the road. "I told you I wanted to show you something."

"In the middle of nowhere?" I glanced around us.

A large hill covered in trees rose above us on the left side of the road, and a lush green meadow spanned the landscape to our right. A calm breeze rustled through the grass.

"Yeah," he answered, climbing off the bike.

I wasn't ready to let him go. All I wanted was to hang onto him tighter, but I reluctantly released him. I stepped onto the pavement and removed the helmet.

"Leave it on the bike," Marek said. "No one will bother it. Come on, it's this way."

Butterflies danced in my stomach when he grabbed my hand.

He didn't seem to notice. He looked both ways before

leading me across the road.

I scanned the sunny landscape as we walked down the shoulder of the road. "Where are you taking me?"

A wide grin spread across his face. "It's right there."

Several paces later, I noticed a break in the trees ahead of us. Slowly, the wonder he'd pointed out began to reveal itself. Piles of rock climbed the hill between the trees, forming a natural staircase. I imagined a waterfall once trickled through the area.

"Let's go." Marek released my hand and began climbing the dry falls.

I followed behind him.

Heaven help me. His ass looked perfect from this angle.

I tried to focus less on that and more on maintaining my footing. I used my hands to pull myself over tall rocks.

I tried to keep up with Marek, but he rushed like he'd done this a million times. He seemed to know exactly where to place his hands and feet to propel him up the hill.

Soon, the rocks became smaller and easier to climb over. I stood upright. I dusted my hands off on my jeans just as we broke through the trees onto a rocky hilltop.

"Where are we—?"

I was stunned into silence when we reached the top of the hill. In front of us spanned the entirety of Eagle Valley. More trees than I ever realized filled the town, and houses of all colors and sizes graced the landscape.

The vibrant green landscape stretched for miles past our small town. I longed to fly above it and explore the gorgeous scenery from new angles.

Up here, the world felt full of possibilities.

Marek lowered himself to the ground and rested his elbows on his knees. I sat beside him.

We gazed out onto Eagle Valley in silence. I noticed the roof of Galen High peeking up through a thick layer of trees at the other end of town. I concentrated close on where I thought the valley was. I spotted a thinning of trees, but it was nearly impossible to see unless you were looking for it.

Marek broke the silence. "Did I mention yet that I'm sorry?"

I turned to him. "Sorry for what?"

Marek raked his fingers through his hair. "I feel terrible about what happened. I never meant to put you in danger. I was supposed to protect you."

My heart sank. I hated to see him so upset.

"It all worked out in the end," I reminded him.

He stared straight ahead, not looking at me. "*This* time. What about the next time you're in danger?"

I shuddered at the thought. "Dorian's gone. I'm not *in* any danger."

Sadness fell across his face when he looked at me. "You can't know that. You have the Power of Grace, Ryn. There are a lot of people who would like to see you dead before you can find Grace and wake her. The demons would love to see the gateways to their realm open again. Right now, you're the only thing standing in their way."

"But they don't even know I *have* the Power of Grace. They don't know a war is coming," I argued.

"You don't know Dorian didn't tell anyone."

I hated to think Marek was right, but as far as I knew, I'd killed everyone Dorian told.

"If Grace is somewhere in Eagle Valley like Fletcher thinks she is, it won't take that long to find her," I pointed out.

Marek raised an eyebrow. "Do you have any clues on where to start?"

I bit my lip. "Well, no. But Eagle Valley isn't very big." I gestured to the town to prove its size.

"Ryn," he said softly. He glanced down at my hand resting on the ground then back up to my eyes.

My cheeks heated under his gaze. "Yeah?"

Marek reached out to slip his fingers into mine. "I want to be there to help you."

The air between us suddenly seemed charged with energy.

"Help me what?" I asked breathlessly.

"Search for Grace. Prevent a bigger war."

I nodded gratefully. "And I trust you'll be there."

It struck me how much I meant it. It'd been a long time since I felt I could count on someone the way I could with Marek.

His eyes danced across my face. "Just promise me something in return."

I fell so deep into his eyes that I practically forgot where I was. My mouth grew dry. "Yeah?"

"Promise me you'll be careful." He spoke so softly that I barely heard him.

"I—I'm not sure I want to be," I heard myself say.

"What do you mean?"

I could feel our bodies inching closer. "Sometimes, Marek, you have to take chances, even when they scare you. Even when the outcome could be as equally amazing as it could be devastating. You never know until you take that chance, until you—"

Marek's lips connected with mine, silencing my words.

In that moment, I forgot what I was going to say. I forgot all about the danger we'd just been discussing. All that seemed to matter were his lips against mine, his fingers tangling themselves in my hair, and my hands running down his back.

My fingers grazed against the scars beneath his shirt. For a moment, I was shocked. Then I only wanted to drag him closer to me, for him to let me kiss him all over and heal whatever emotional pain he'd been through. I knew trying to erase his past would be futile, but in that moment, I thought maybe I had the power to help the boy I'd seen in my dream.

Marek pulled me even closer. His tongue grazed across my bottom lip.

Good lord. This was even better than flying.

Far too soon, we parted.

For a moment, all seemed well in the world, but I couldn't help but hear Marek's words echo in my mind.

This time.

This time, things *had* turned out okay, but I couldn't shake the feeling that Marek was right. There was going to be a *next time.* And I had the strangest feeling that next time would be even worse. We'd only just won the first fight.

I knew what lay ahead was going to be a very long battle.

END OF BOOK ONE

This story will continue in book two of the Divine Fate Trilogy, *Touched by Grace.*

ABOUT THE AUTHOR

Alicia Rades is a USA Today bestselling author of young adult and new adult paranormal fiction. When she's not dreaming up magical stories, she's either binge-watching paranormal TV shows, meditating, or spending time with her family. She has an unhealthy obsession with psychic characters and writes with a deck of tarot cards next to her computer.